When seventeen-year-old Ingrid Harper realizes she may not have the talent to pursue a scholarship for the most prestigious art school in Australia, she turns to pink hair dye as a distraction.

Her new hair captures the attention of a fellow art student, Kat, who introduces Ingrid to the LGBT clubbing scene, and although Ingrid enjoys partying with her new friend, she becomes caught up in confusion about her sexuality. Her fear is overwhelming—she can't think about anything else.

Until her best friend, Summer, reveals that she is pregnant.

As her best friend faces the realities of being pregnant at seventeen, Ingrid is shown the true definition of courage. It motivates her to come out about her sexuality—she likes girls. Only girls. Now she just has to work out what that means for the other areas of her life.

A NineStar Press Publication

SunFire Imprint

Published by NineStar Press
P.O. Box 91792,
Albuquerque, New Mexico, 87199 USA.
www.ninestarpress.com

Sweethearts

Copyright © 2018 by Gemma Gilmore
Cover Art by Natasha Snow Copyright © 2018

This is a work of fiction. Names, characters, places, and incidents are either the product of the author's imagination or are used fictitiously. Any resemblance to actual persons living or dead, business establishments, events, or locales is entirely coincidental.

All rights reserved. No part of this publication may be reproduced in any material form, whether by printing, photocopying, scanning or otherwise without the written permission of the publisher. To request permission and all other inquiries, contact NineStar Press at the physical or web addresses above or at Contact@ninestarpress.com.

Printed in the USA
First Edition
January, 2018

Print ISBN: 978-1-947904-96-5

Also available in eBook, ISBN: 978-1-947904-92-7

Warning: This book contains depictions of underage drinking.

SWEETHEARTS

Gemma Gilmore

For my sister, Shannon, who inspires me, challenges me, and reminds
me to never stop dreaming.

Acknowledgements

Thank you to my family: my mum, Bas, who has been my partner in crime since day one, and my best friend, Lucy—you are my motivators. Thank you to everybody at NineStar Press, the editors and copy editors. Most importantly, thank you for reading my words.

Chapter One

I AM DESPERATELY trying not to attract attention.

My arms are folded across my chest. My chin is tucked into my neck. I am leaning against the brick wall as I watch her sing. It takes every ounce of strength I have to keep my face still, hiding any expression that bubbles to the surface. Any reaction I have to her lilting voice is shoved down, adding to the pit in my stomach.

The younger students are sitting respectfully in their seats. They are still too naive to question the teachers when they are told they must be present. I know better than to think that this school performance is anything special to Amber Freeman. She's been singing since before she could walk, and although I am always the first viewer, her YouTube videos are gaining more and more popularity with every upload. This is just practice to her. A warm-up.

The spotlights are trained on her, and she throws her hands up whilst the climax of the song cascades from her talented lips. I let my eyes flicker shut and Amber's voice surrounds me, caressing my ears as she sings deeply. Her voice is crashing through me, tingling across the skin on my arms and seeping through my body, calming me.

My head has fallen back against the wall, and I remain frozen there as I listen to her sing. In this moment, nothing else matters. With my eyes closed, she's right next to me. Singing softly, untying the knot that's sunken deep into that pit in the bottom of my stomach.

"Ingrid? What the hell are you doing?" The voice that hisses right next to my ear jerks me out of my daydream.

I jump with shock and wrench my eyes open, tearing myself away from the peaceful moment. In front of me, my best friend Summer stands, her arms folded across her chest and her eyes wide in that *you are busted* expression.

"Jesus," I mutter. "I thought you had better things to do than sneak up on people. Way to give me a heart attack."

"I thought you had better things to do than stand here creepily at the back of the gym listening to Amber sing," Summer challenges me, an amused smile dancing across her full lips.

"You snuck up on me and you're calling *me* the creep?" I snort. "Come on, let's get out of here."

The quicker I can get Summer outside of this gym, the quicker I can shove away the fact that she caught me watching Amber's performance. We duck behind the last row of seating and out of the door in the corner of the room, swiftly ignoring the *Emergency Exit Only* sign. We've done this so many times now that it's like second nature.

Outside, the rain lashes against the building. The wind howls so loudly that I'm surprised no one noticed our little escape from the gymnasium—then again, they never do. For Summer, there's more to life than just sitting in a desk at school. Any chance my best friend has to escape the mundane restrictions of life is an opportunity she must take. She's never been the kind of girl to follow the traditional paths.

Then again, neither have I.

My thoughts still spin as we duck through the car park and head out to the tin shed at the back of the school. Summer knew exactly where to find me during Amber's performance. She knows that I watch Amber. While everyone else in our grade snuck off to make out in abandoned classrooms or smoke cigarettes behind the main building, I followed the crowd into the gymnasium with one intention.

Why did I need to watch her?

"I had a headache and the gym was dark." I shrug off Summer's curious expression as we take shelter under the tin roof. The rain really lashes down now, bouncing off the pavement and whipping through the trees. "It was better than watching you make out with Jackson for an hour straight."

My snide comment is low but, right now, I'll do anything to take the attention away from me.

"You had a headache, so you decided to listen to Amber sing?" Summer rolls her eyes at me. "Makes sense."

She fidgets with her oversized tartan scarf, staring out into the rain. Maybe I'm not the only one who is trying to avoid things today.

"You were in there too," I argue half-heartedly. "What's your obsession with her?"

This time, Summer does turn to me. "*I'm* obsessed?" She snorts. "Ingrid, honey, if I'm obsessed, then you're deranged."

"Then I'm deranged."

Summer rolls her eyes, signalling the end of that particular conversation. "Whatever. Your deeply disturbing issues are the least of my problems right now. Look, Ingrid, I think I'm going to have to take a test."

Red splotches gleam against Summer's pale cheeks, and I watch her carefully. She tugs on that scarf like it's strangling her.

"Like an STD test?"

"Are you stupid?" I know her voice is harsher than intended, and I brush it off with a blunt laugh. "A pregnancy test."

"Oh, for god's sake, here we go again. You and Jackson really need to invest in some efficient birth control because this *I'm pregnant* freak-out that you have every month is getting boring."

"Trust me, I know." Her tone is suddenly tense, and she blinks back emotion. "But right now, I'm pretty sure I have the devil's spawn growing inside of me, so I'm allowed to freak out. I'm two weeks late."

I raise my eyebrows. She's never been *this* late before. "Jackson is *not* the devil's spawn. You know he loves you. But I highly doubt you're pregnant. It's all the stress from thinking you're pregnant every month starting to get to you."

"Yeah, okay, whatever." She says, throwing her hands up in defeat. "I knew I shouldn't have said anything. I don't know what you're moping about—we got a free class and you got to watch Amber singing. It's a damn good day for Ingrid Harper right now."

"Listen, I really did just have a headache. I don't care about Amber's singing. And you and Jackson *were* quite obviously distracted. You didn't seem to have pregnancy on your mind during that public make-out session. Or maybe you did. Either way, I think it's a damn good day for both of us, don't you think?"

I know what Summer is doing. She is the ultimate denier of reality. More than that, she is aware that I will follow along with every topic change she throws at me. I get distracted easily, apparently.

Summer laughs, but the smile doesn't quite reach her eyes. Distraction is inevitable right now, for both of us. These are not issues we should be faced with at seventeen years old. Summer's mother is getting married soon, so that's just one more thing to top off what I'm coining *Summer's Distressing Summer*.

We stand silently as the rain pours over the sides of the flimsy tin roof. Muddy water pools right to the edges of the door. It's mid-December. While politicians are throwing around the term *climate change* like it's currency, I stare at the pools of water near this emergency exit, wondering if our town has sufficient flood safety plans.

"Come over tonight," she murmurs. "Please, Ingrid."

"You're buying me McDonald's." I sigh in return. The truth is, I have my own things to worry about, whether Summer is pregnant or not. She's been with Jackson for three years—that's three years they have successfully been together and prevented pregnancy. It's not a possibility. It just isn't.

Summer is wild, just like her name. Her light-brown hair is constantly tangled, but her dominating blue eyes seem to distract everyone.

But today, she looks out at the grey sky and nervously chews at her lip, clutching that damn scarf so tightly that I know she's already certain about this pregnancy. More so than I've ever seen before. Her blue eyes don't seem so bright today.

"I heard Jackson was thinking about transferring to the art school. I didn't think that boy had an artistic bone in his body." I smirk, desperately trying to relax Summer. I don't know what to say when she's so shut off like this. My lie is smooth, slipping off my lips easily.

"Yeah, he does comics. I don't know, I guess they're funny."

"It's our last year of high school. Surely he's left it a bit late?" I frown in earnest now.

What Summer doesn't know is that I've known Jackson a lot longer than she has. I know that he's been wanting to do art since he started high school, but his military-driven father would never allow it—he's all about physical education, mathematics, and science. He used to drill that into Jackson every time I was around; *none of this fairy fluff nonsense*, he would say pointedly.

"Look, Ingrid, I don't really want to talk about Jackson right now," Summer snaps, finally releasing the titan grip on her checked scarf and running a frustrated hand through her frizzy hair.

"Do you even want me to stay tonight then?" I throw back. "I can't deal with you when you're being like this. Either let me in or let me go. I've got shit to do."

To my complete surprise, Summer snorts as she turns to face me. "Just shut up and come and sleep over at my house. I need your brutal honesty, but I also need you to do literally everything I say right now. You know I'd do the same for you."

I don't bother telling her that to be in her position, I'd actually have to get closer than two feet to a guy, but I think she already knows that.

"Look, I don't like that you called Jackson the devil before. I don't care if he's annoying sometimes, if you are...pregnant...it's definitely not the devil's spawn that could be growing inside of you. And that's all I'm going to say about that," I huff.

"Okay, I didn't know you were Jackson's number-one cheerleader, but whatever."

"Yeah, whatever."

IN SUMMER'S DARK bedroom, the computer screen is the only thing I can see. I read the caption as I wait for the video to load. *Uploaded 3 minutes ago.* I'm right on schedule, but it's not intentional. I know Summer won't be back from McDonald's for at least another fifteen minutes—twenty if that hot guy is working on the counter again.

And then suddenly, Amber Freeman is in front of me, singing her heart out. Her eyes are scrunched up as her voice wavers. It's a beautiful song, of sadness and hope and disappointment. It's a song I know all too well, a song that is pulling at my heartstrings, making me clench my fists as the tears threaten to spill over. It fills my ears and captures my attention, leaving me frozen.

As Amber's voice crashes in my headphones, sending shivers through my body, I ignore the world. I ignore Summer's chaotic household; I ignore the silence of my phone—shoving persistent concerns of her lack of contact out of my mind. All we needed was a Big Mac. She'll be back soon.

My hands are stained pink as my knuckles tighten and Amber's song reaches its climax. It's beautiful. To put herself out there, showing the world her deepest, naked self... It's courageous. It's admirable. It's amazing.

I'm crying as her lilting lyrics caress my ears. The beat slows; her strong voice softens as the final crescendo of music dances over her. I watch the intricate hand gestures, the way her brown eyes tighten as she forces out a note higher and bursting with more emotion than the last. The way she holds herself, briefly swaying with the music before falling into the final verse.

My body is taut as the screen fades to black, and I only let my breath come out in small bursts until the explosion of emotions crashing inside me subsides. With shaking fingers, I pull open the comment box.

It seems foreign now. It has been so long since I've provided any evidence that I even knew these videos existed. I'm not going to sit around and pretend that everything is okay. It's not.

Have I ever even been *just* okay? Was there ever even a time when I actually felt content in my life? I don't even know what happy feels like anymore. I'm just constantly broken.

It's that thought that pounds all the way to my fingertips, causing them to rush across the keyboard. The tapping echoes across the room, mixing in with my shallow breathing.

My heart pounds as my fingers halt. My mouse hovers over the Submit button. I've long since changed my username, but my display picture is always the same. Amber would know straight away who this comment is from—especially considering it would be the only one there. There is no running now.

"Ingrid?"

For a second, I'm frozen, and then quicker than I know is possible, I shut down all evidence of Amber Freeman ever being present on my computer screen, abandoning my comment. I'm not crying anymore. I'm just red. Red-faced is okay. I can deal with that.

"Well, that's the last time I ever check my spam box," I stammer. "I thought you said you had internet security."

"Right, you needed headphones to check your spam box?" Summer asks sceptically, throwing her body down next to mine and shoving a bag of hot McDonald's in front of my face. "I need to keep the lights off. If we eat in the dark, the calories don't count. But don't pretend I didn't notice that your hair is pink. You stole my hair dye, bitch. I was saving that for the day that Jackson and I inevitably break up and I have the mental breakdown of the century."

"I don't care if the calories count or not." I laugh, shoving a fry into my mouth to hide my shaking hands. "I have no one to impress. Hence, the pink hair."

"I guess it looks better on you, anyway. And I'm gonna get really fat soon, so neither of us will be impressing anyone."

"You took the test?" I breathe. My heart rate had just begun getting back to normal, and suddenly, it's hammering in my chest again.

"Yeah, in a goddamn McDonald's bathroom. It was one of the cheap ones, though, so I don't really believe it. I'm going to buy another one tomorrow."

"It said you were pregnant?"

"It wasn't clear." She sighs, seemingly annoyed at my question. "Just drop it."

"You brought it up!" I argue.

"And I'm shutting it down! Just eat your Big Mac and tell me that I'm beautiful, no matter what, please. I'm not pestering you about whatever you were doing on your computer before, so can you please just do this for me?"

"You're beautiful no matter what." I grin, taking a bite out of my burger.

"WHY ARE YOU being weird?"

I almost choke on my eggs benedict as Jackson throws the question at me accusingly. I've never been good at keeping secrets, but I was enjoying the quietness and there's no one else I'd rather be eating eggs benedict with at four in the afternoon.

"I'm not being weird," I retort. "You're being weird."

"No, I'm not. What's going on, Ingrid? Why haven't you mentioned Summer yet? You always have something to bitch about. I know she's the one who forced you to dye your hair that ridiculous colour."

"She didn't *force* me." I start, but there is no point arguing with him. Pink hair dye would be right on top of the list of Summer's crazy ideas, so I don't blame him for jumping to conclusions. "Look, I was watching something last night, and I think she caught me."

Jackson's face lights up. "Porn?" I don't miss the hopeful tone that escapes his smirking lips.

"You're disgusting. Not porn. Worse."

"Amber."

"Yes. Amber."

"God, Ingrid. You need to quit her already. It's messing up your life."

"I can't," I groan. "Summer told me yesterday that I have deeply disturbing issues. She caught me watching Amber's performance at school. I mean, to be fair, you two were eating each other's faces and I had nothing better to do, but I'm starting to think that she's right."

"Ingrid, I'm going to ask you something and you can't get mad at me, okay?" Jackson chews at his full lips in a way that immediately takes me back to the first year of high school.

Summer didn't know either of us back then, but we knew each other. Those full lips would find themselves smashing against mine behind every building, inside every cleaning closet, under the overgrown willow tree at the bottom of the oval...

And every time, as his eager hands inched up my ridiculously short skirt, I would push them away and he would respectfully chuckle and continue kissing me. It never went further. It only lasted six months. Summer doesn't *ever* need to know.

But he was my best friend during that time, and I know him well enough to know that he's about to ask me about something that I'd rather not go into. He's got that look of caution clouding behind his features—the caution that only comes when he's about to hurt my feelings.

"Go ahead." I sigh, staring at my half-finished eggs.

"Are you...like..." He groans and tries to start the sentence again. "When we were...messing around or whatever, back when we were fifteen...you never let it get any further. Sure, you were a good kisser, but...you never got into it." He scrunches his eyes shut as if protecting himself as he launches into his question. "Are you a lesbian, Ingrid?"

I choke on my laugh, completely disarming my defensive stance. I don't know what kind of question I was expecting from Jackson—maybe something about Summer, maybe something about our own history—but this was *not* it.

My heart is hammering, and my tongue is dry. Suddenly, my hands shake so violently that my fork falls onto my plate with a loud clatter.

Jackson stares at me, an amused smirk suddenly growing on his lips. All traces of nerves are taken away by my dramatic reaction. I cough loudly, attempting to gather my thoughts.

"You're ridiculous," I hiss. I'm furious, but he is still grinning at me.

"You're obsessed with Amber Freeman," he throws back casually.

"I'm not—" I cut myself off because I *know* I am fascinated by her. It's those videos and the drama that seems to follow her everywhere...

But it's just to pass the time and ignore the rest of the vapid characters in our school. "I'm not a lesbian."

The words sound so unconvincing, even to me, but they are the truth. The weakness in my voice and the pressure in my chest is because Jackson caught me off guard, not because I'm lying.

I'm not lying.

"Fine, fine. Whatever. But you are acting really weird today, so don't kill me for thinking something was up."

I'm about to use my only defence and tell him that something *is* most definitely up and that maybe he should be eating with his girlfriend, because she's eating for two now, but I snap my mouth shut.

Instead, I roll my eyes, feeling satisfied as my wall of cool rolls down. I am calm. I am cool.

I am *not* a lesbian.

OF ALL THE reactions to my bright pink hair, there is only one that shocks me to my very core. Summer pretended to be surprised and the rest of our friends followed suit, one of them announcing that my hair looks like a pink marshmallow.

Some of the boys appraise me with raised eyebrows and slight arousal in their features. Most don't seem to care all that much.

It is Amber Freeman, however, that reacts most dramatically—which, in itself, isn't at all surprising. I had been expecting a longwinded rant about the latest boy drama to happen in her life, but when Amber first sees me striding into the classroom, she squeaks. I turn to her with raised eyebrows, feeling amused as her brown eyes practically bulge out of her head.

"Ingrid, I..." She stumbles over her words as they die in her throat, before walking over to me. Without asking, or even hesitating, she runs her fingers through my hair. My breath catches in my throat, and I swear I catch Amber licking her lips. "It looks great."

It takes me a moment to compose myself, but when I do, I roll my eyes. "Whatever."

Summer stares at me, mouth open. Only I notice the redness in her eyes that has been there since Friday. I bite my lip, trying to suppress the giddy smile that wants to rise from brushing Amber off. I am happy to distract Summer for a little while. That's what she needs right now.

Amber dismisses my flippant remark and marches straight back to her seat, seemingly oblivious to the chatters that surround us. I take my seat next to Summer and sigh loudly.

"Jackson wants to go to a party this weekend," Summer murmurs. The chaos in the classroom drowns out our hushed conversation, and I turn to face Summer directly. We still have twenty minutes before class starts, and this is important.

"You need to tell him," I say sharply.

Of course, she can't go to a party. Summer is well known for her antics at Port Macquarie's parties. She drinks way too much and ends up doing something completely crazy, becoming the highlight of the night for everyone.

The last party that she went to, she ran out of the boy's house—I don't even remember whose party it was because Summer completely stole the show—and jumped onto one of the boats that was docked on the wharf that night. Of course, she was far too drunk to do anything on the boat, but it ended with her throwing up all over the deck and sleeping in it. No one knew about it until we heard the screams of the owners the next morning. Thankfully for Summer, we were all there, somewhat reluctantly, to help her clean it.

"I took another one. It was, uh, it was definitely positive," she says. I don't know if Summer is confirming that she already told Jackson and he didn't take it well, but my head snaps up and I am yanked out of my memories of drunken nights and drama. The blood has drained from my best friend's face, and my sigh bubbles up inside of me before I can stop it.

"You weren't being careful enough." My chiding is not needed here, and I realise this when Summer's face crumples. I snap my mouth shut as Summer attempts to compose herself, going unnoticed by our classmates. I don't ask her anything else because right now she needs the silence.

Right now, she needs me.

"I ASSUME YOU'LL be coming to Cloud Nine tonight, Pinkie?"

My head snaps up when a silence settles over the scattered group of art students milling around behind the gym. I come out here to think, and usually they just ignore me, but today, they seem fascinated by my pink hair.

I'm not used to the nickname, but of course, I'm not used to the bubble-gum pink locks that wrestle with my cheekbones.

"What's Cloud Nine?" I ask hesitantly. Apparently, all I needed to finally fit in here was a little bit of hair dye.

I've been in the arts faculty for three years now and never received any attention from my fellow arts students. I guess my sandy-blonde hair and timid attitude were too tame for them.

"Oh, baby, you've got a lot to learn." It's a tall brunette with a tongue piercing that speaks.

I eye her carefully and can't help but appreciate her courage in outfit choices. She wears a tight black tank top that shows a good portion of her well-developed abs, a bright-green belly-button piercing, and even tighter blue jeans. In her dark-brown hair, she wears bright-blue streaks.

"Meet me at the bus stop in town at eight if you want a taste of heaven."

I blush furiously as the girl flashes me a confident smile, licking her red lips. Her gaze is a little more intense when she looks at me, compared to the looks she gives the other girls and boys standing around. If I didn't know any better, I could almost say she's coming on to me.

I swallow dryly when I realise that I don't actually know any better.

"CLOUD NINE... YOU'RE kidding right?" Maybe it's the fact that I just heard Summer throwing up over the phone, but her voice sounds...odd.

"Just tell me what I should wear," I moan, staring blankly into my wardrobe. "You're always good at this kind of stuff."

"Ingrid, sweetie, do you know *anything* about Cloud Nine?" The sudden sympathetic lilt to Summer's voice terrifies me.

I nervously utter, "No?"

"Oh god, okay, sit down for a second."

"Why?" I frown, running my hands over a silver minidress.

"Just do it," Summer snaps.

I can almost *see* her rolling her eyes on the other end of the phone. Feeling sceptical, I collapse onto my bed, kick off my shoes, and stare into the wardrobe.

"Okay, are you sitting down?"

"Yes. What are you going to tell me? What's so—"

"Cloud Nine is a gay club." Summer's voice hitches with narcissistic glee. Pregnancy hasn't taken away her inner mean girl, it seems. "Particularly catered for those of ah...feminine preferences."

"You mean...?" My voice is robotic. I can't even *begin* to comprehend the way my stomach jolts when Summer speaks next.

"Ingrid, honey, you're going to a lesbian club." Summer snorts.

Chapter Two

I'M NOT SUPPOSED to be here.

That's my first thought as I scratch at my ridiculous fishnet stockings. Summer, it seems, has more important things on her mind than helping me dress appropriately for sneaking into a lesbian club—and hey, I can't blame her. Unfortunately, it's left me standing uncomfortably on the corner near the bus stop, waiting for that girl. Kate, Kath, Kal...? *God*, I can't even remember her name.

Of course, over the phone, Summer's distracted outfit suggestions seemed logical—and even thoughtful. Standing here, under the harsh street light, I contemplate the silver high heels and black shift—okay, so it's more like a shirt. I sent a picture to Summer for confirmation, and my loud-mouthed best friend proudly announced that if she swung my way, she'd totally "bang" me.

My stomach lurched at that comment, and I'm not sure if it's become unstuck from just below my windpipe ever since. My hot-pink hair is free and messy and the bright-red lipstick feels dry on my lips.

Just as I begin to wonder if my oblivious parents will even notice my disappearance tonight, a strong smell of smoke—and something that is *definitely* stronger than tobacco—has me glancing around.

"Pinkie, you showed!" She sounds surprised, and to my own surprise, she is alone. "Maybe you've got more potential than I thought?" Her smirk widens as she openly checks me out, letting her gaze linger on my stocking-clad legs. I shift uncomfortably under her scrutiny.

"What...what was your name again?" I ask, cringing as the girl slouches an easy arm over me and begins walking me down an obscure alleyway. "And, uh, where are you taking me? I thought we were going to a club..."

I take my own opportunity to look the girl up and down, noticing her dramatic outfit. If I thought she looked good before, behind the gym, it was nothing compared to how she's scrubbed up now.

Her brown hair falls loose in a surprisingly Amber Freeman–esque style, and I wonder if that's why I suddenly think that she's more attractive.

I don't consider that thought for too long.

Her tight blue dress accentuates every curve on her toned body—and the blue in her dress makes the blue streaks in her hair look even brighter. There is something about her sparkly eye makeup that makes it hard for me to look away. It's mesmerising in the way it shines under the small-town lights.

"My name's Katrina," she replies, lazily letting her cigarette hang between her lips. "But you'll call me Kat, okay? And we *are* going to the club. Just relax, Pinkie." She takes in my worried expression and smirks. "Well, we aren't exactly going to get in through the front with you, Newbie. I hardly see you as the type to carry around a fake ID."

I nod, embarrassed, and Kat's grin grows even wider.

"Watch and learn, sister."

She takes one last drag of her cigarette before stomping it out with her oversized army boot. Kicking twice at a door that hides, half-obscured by the graffiti laden wall, Kat shouts, "Buster, it's me. K plus one."

I jump a little when the door swings open, bringing with it the bitter scent of sweat and alcohol. My eyebrows shoot up when I realise that Buster is a petite bouncer with a dark cap and black overalls—I would never have picked the slight woman with tattoos spread across both arms and like snakes curling across her chest, to be employed as a bouncer in this busy club. But as she gives me a once-over with fierce green eyes and an even fiercer snarl curling on her upper lip, I don't doubt for a second that she could handle her own in a fight.

I'm about to speak—although, the words are tangled in my throat despite my urge not to seem impolite—but my attention is locked on the pounding club scene in front of me, and for the first time in my life, I am rendered completely speechless.

Of course, I *tell* myself that the sudden dryness in my mouth has absolutely *nothing* to do with the women throwing themselves over poles, swaying to the suddenly erotic music, flashing cheeky grins to the clubgoers as they rid themselves of another piece of clothing. I force myself not to stare at the women grinding against each other or the few men that palm themselves through their jeans as they watch the scene in front of them.

Suddenly, my heart is pounding and I can't believe I am here, and *god,* why don't I want to leave yet? I should be running a thousand miles. I should be disgusted and horrified, but I can't, for the life of me, even bring myself to look away.

"No need to start salivating yet, Newbie. We're just getting started." Kat winks at me, grabbing loosely at my hand again. This girl really doesn't have a problem with personal space. "Let's get you a drink. I can tell you've never been here before—you've probably never been to a normal club, even!" She lets out a booming laugh as if that's the most hysterical thing she's ever heard and drags me past Buster and through the grinding women. "Well, let me tell you, this ain't a normal club. This is a night that you're never going to forget."

I struggle to keep up with what she is saying—and I tell myself very firmly that this has *nothing* to do with the brunette stripper who has just stripped off her tight white shirt to reveal a pair of very perky breasts and everything to do with the fact that Kat talks at an unnaturally fast speed that only the likes of Amber Freeman could keep up with.

For a moment, I think about Amber standing in a club like this, surrounded by aroused men and even more aroused women. The thought is so ridiculous that a bark of laughter erupts in my throat, and as Kat pulls me to the counter of the bar, ordering me a lime vodka, I am reduced to a fit of giggles.

"So, Pinkie, do you have a boyfriend?" Kat leans against the bar, watching me laugh with an amused smile. She quirks an eyebrow and leans even closer. "A girlfriend?" she purrs.

"I—" I blush and choke a little on the thick, smoggy air of the club. "No. I'm single."

"Good to know." She smirks. "TJ is working the bar tonight, so feel free to have as many drinks as you like—he always has my back."

TJ wears a gold hoop earring in his right ear and a turquoise nose stud. His dreadlocks are pulled back with a silver headscarf that contrasts with his dark skin. He winks at me as he hands me a drink, shouting something incomprehensible over the pounding music. I nod and smile back, as if I have any clue what he is saying to me.

We down our drinks quickly, eager to get out on the dance floor. TJ watches us for a while. I let my gaze roam around the booming club. The fact that a place like this exists in my tiny, conservative town is overwhelming.

It goes against everything I've ever known, everything my careless parents have forced onto me. In this moment, I am not afraid to admit that I love it. I love the ecstasy crackling in the air and the way I feel like someone else. I don't know who I am in here, but I'm sure as hell not Ingrid Harper anymore.

Too many drinks and a lot of laughter later, we are in the abyss of the dance floor, and when Kat points out how tense I look, I make a promise to myself to be less tense. This is one random Tuesday night, this one experience—I *will* make the most of it.

Sweaty bodies pound against each other, rocking in time with the music, losing themselves in the mass of people. All types of sloppy embraces happen around us. People of all types, all genders come together on this one dance floor, to this one song, in this tiny town, and I belong here.

I am so used to holding myself together, being composed, being harsh, hiding my feelings with an abrasive surface, not afraid to cut. When I watch how happy these people look, how absolutely carefree they are and how easy it is for them to just let go completely, I realise I want that too. I don't want to care anymore.

So, when Kat encircles me sloppily with her arms around my waist, I let it happen. In the limbo between tipsy and drunk, I've never felt better. The music is blood pounding through my veins. It is the way that Kat digs her fingernails into my exposed skin and the way I lean forward, letting my head rest on her shoulder, swaying with the music.

"Jesus, Pinkie."

The song is reaching a climax and fists are pumping. I am sweating and my head is spinning and my heart is pounding, and, *god*, I can't seem to catch my breath. Kat laughs in my ear—not the booming laugh I heard earlier in the night, but a husky drunken chuckle that I am sure is only meant for my ears.

We dance, oblivious as people fall clumsily to the floor, as they stumble off to have drunken sex in the alleyway outside. We dance until our feet hurt, until our eyes droop and the consistent throbbing in my body becomes too much to manage.

"C'mon, doll, let's get you home." Kat is slurring now—whether it is because she's too drunk or too tired to speak properly, I don't know, because I'm too drunk to wonder. TJ waves goodbye as we stumble out of the club, and I blow a kiss in his direction.

It is only when we are out on the starkly dark street, stumbling through crowds of screaming friends, sneering boys, and crying girls that I realise I cannot go home.

"I'm too drunk," I mumble into Kat's shoulder. "My parents... Kat, they can't think I've...been to a gay club."

"D'you have anyone to call?" Kat murmurs into my hair.

I think about it for a long moment before fishing my phone out of my bra and dialling the only number I can remember in my drunken state.

THE ONLY REASON my drunk mind remembers his number is because that's the only time I used to call him—when I was so drunk that my teeth felt numb and my toes vibrated. When I was so drunk that his kisses felt like oxygen and I could only grip him so hard before he shattered in my arms.

"Are you *sure* you're not a lesbian?" Jackson smirks down at me from his tiny bed. I flop against a pillow on his carpeted floor, drunkenly trying to meet his eyes.

"I don't think *you* get to ask *me* those kinds of questions anymore," I mumble, ignoring the bubbles slimily bumping through my stomach. "Thanks for letting me stay."

"Why don't I get to ask you those questions?"

Despite my drunken state, I can feel Jackson staring hard at me.

"Since when did you turn into Miss Defensive?"

"Since you got my best friend pregnant and decided to be a real jerk about it." I can see myself drunkenly slamming him with my words—I *will* be the winner of this conversation.

Silence engulfs me and my eyes droop shut. The bubbles in my stomach dance up to my head and it feels amazing.

"What did you just say?" Jackson's hard voice bursts the bubbles, jolting me awake and slamming like a brick on my chest.

Why does he sound so—

"What the *hell* did you just say?"

—shocked?

"Ahh..." My breath comes harshly, and I force myself into a sitting position, grasping my shaking fingers together. "Ahh..."

"Summer's pregnant?"

It slams into me. I gasp for air. *I fucked up. I fucked up.* My heart thunders and the dark room is too hot. How did I manage to mess this up? What is wrong with me?

"Jackson, I'm drunk. I'm sorry, I..."

"You're lying?" Jackson asks, his eyes glowing with anger. "Is that your excuse? You're drunk? Maybe that'll do. Cut the crap, Ingrid. Spit it out."

My mouth is so dry. I don't think I could speak even if I wanted to. Memories flash in my foresight. Kat is dancing; I am drinking; TJ is smirking. I lick a shot from Kat's neck. She grips my waist tighter, laughing with me. Amber Freeman flashes in front of my eyes. I wanted to be with her tonight.

My stomach heaves.

I open my mouth, desperate to say something—*anything* at all would be nice—and that's when I throw up all over Jackson's bedroom floor.

PEOPLE LOOK AT me differently now. Eyes follow me, lustful gazes and lowered lashes. Boys and girls watch me, from ahead and behind, as I stride down the hallway, chin raised with a hand on my hip. It's not just the pink hair. I know that.

I hide my terror. I hide it in my grungy outfit and consistent scowl. I hide it in my sneer and the way I shove past first years without saying *excuse me.* I walk towards the art room with purpose. If I keep walking, I will not fall. If I keep walking, Summer will not find me.

I am terrified. I left Jackson's house as soon as I woke up, ignoring the wafting smell of bleach and harsh cleaning chemical that filled his room. My drunken slip-up has probably cost me my best friend.

"...Ingrid?"

My head whips around at a speed that cracks my neck. *No.* It's not Summer, but the lurching of my stomach makes me wish it was. Amber Freeman stands in front of me with huge brown eyes, clutching her bag strap, filled with hopes and dreams and all of the things I loathe in her.

"What the hell do *you* want?" I snap. If I yell, she doesn't hear the shaking in my voice. She can interpret my sudden, sharp intake of breath as anger.

She doesn't cringe. Amber doesn't even flinch at my harsh words. "I...I heard Summer talking about you in class. She was mad. I don't know what you did, but she's not happy."

I sneer. It hides the flash of hurt that thunders inside of me. It hides the way my lips remain dry in Amber's presence. A gentle blush creeps across her cheeks, and I put it down to intimidation. She's scared of me. Of course, she is. She has to be.

"So? It's fine. Summer is fine."

Amber presses her lips together in that *I don't believe you* expression that I know so well. I know it because I've studied it. For hours and hours. When I'm meant to be finishing my reading for English or working on a scientific report. When I'm meant to be studying colour theory or working on my art portfolio. That's when I allow myself to steal those glances. That's when I memorise every inch of her face. The exact curve of her lips, the sparkle in her eyes. I've seen every expression dance across her face.

In those moments, when I'm watching her, that's when I have no control.

"I was, uh. Well, I wanted to know if I could speak to you. As friends. You know, alone," she mumbles.

A few things happen at once. The first being, my heart rate picks up considerably. The thudding in my chest is so hard, so intense that I'm sure she can see it under my thin white shirt that I found at the bottom of my bag this morning. The second being that Kat walks past. She's openly staring at me before wolf-whistling, throwing me a wink, and sashaying her hips as she turns into the art classroom.

"I..." My heart is still pounding—god, *why*?—and I can't seem to swallow all the saliva in my mouth. "We're not friends."

"Ingrid. Please." There it is. I roll my eyes at Amber's plea. I tell myself that the acceleration of my heartbeat has absolutely nothing to do with Amber's prolonged eye contact.

"Fine." I cut her off before she can say anything else.

I don't know how I end up in Amber Freeman's bedroom. I trace back the events leading to this very moment as I attempt to understand exactly how Amber dragged me here. She talks so fast, using so many words to say so little. I am so hung-over that I feel disconnected from the world. There is a pause before every reaction. A moment of traction before my body can catch up and realise what exactly is going on.

At the time, it seemed so much easier to just agree, to get to the point. As I eye the soft toys piled at the end of her bed with mild amusement, it becomes apparent that Amber is yet to reach that point.

The girl in question is perched nervously on the edge of her desk, next to her pink computer. She isn't speaking, but her knee bounces up and down, distracting me. She wears a short navy-blue dress and heavy army boots. I'd taunted her about those boots just six months ago, relentless sneering, sarcastic comments...

It terrifies me to think that, despite my harsh words, she continues wearing them. She is not going to change her eccentric ways for anyone—unlike me, who, until recently, has followed the sheep just to survive through the social hierarchy that is high school.

"Obviously, I wanted to talk to you about why you feel the need to be so damn rude to me all the time," Amber bursts out, causing me to whip my head around. "That's why I suggested we come to my house. We have an hour left for lunch, and I'm sure no one will miss me."

"I—"

"I only want to speak with you as a *friend*, Ingrid," Amber emphasises, continuing to hold my gaze for unusually long. "I'm not your competitor. I'm not against you. I don't want to fight."

"You're ridiculous." I smirk. "You know that, right?"

Amber presses her full lips together, fiddling with the hair tie that remains wrapped around her wrist.

"I'm not ridiculous," she argues. "I mean, *you're* the ridiculous one. You've bullied me for years. Since day care, if my parent's stories are anything to go by. It doesn't get to me. So you keep going. That's ridiculous."

"I don't bully you." It's a defence and a lie. I am a bully. I'm a bitch. And I've treated Amber horribly since the moment I met her. "I do it because I feel sorry for you. You're so dramatic. You need it."

What does that even mean, idiot? As soon as the words tumble out of my mouth, I want to snatch them up and run for the hills. I'm mortified. *This* is why I don't speak to her. When she's around, my words are misshapen. When she's around, all I can do is watch her full lips as she talks.

"You know, I can tell when you're lying, Ingrid."

"How?" I ask, raising my eyebrow sceptically. I don't want Amber trying to get into my head more than she already can.

"You do this thing when you aren't telling the truth. I see you doing it all the time."

"What *thing*?" I snap.

"Your eyes. They flicker upwards and you chew your bottom lip. Also, you scratch the back of your neck—but only if you're really trying to hide something."

"I do *not*!" I splutter.

"You do," Amber insists. "*Look*, you're doing it now!"

I jerk my arm back—which was absent-mindedly scratching at the soft skin behind my hot pink hair. God, what is wrong with this girl?

"You can beg all you want." The rest of the words remain stale on my tongue as I realise the potential double meaning of that questionable sentence, but I shake my head and push forward. "We're not friends. We never were. We never will be. I'm sorry about being rude to you, but we just can't get along. I guess you're just a great singer and I'm jealous."

Bile rises in my throat and I snap my mouth shut. It's not the hangover that leaves my stomach heaving and my chest hammering. It's the truth. It's telling Amber the truth. By admitting this, she knows I watch her videos. She knows that I have hung around in the back of those ridiculous gymnasium performances. Only Summer knew that. And now she knows it.

"You shine, Ingrid. When you watch me singing...I watch you shine." It's a mumble. Not a dramatic whisper or an overemphasised statement—it's not forced or rehearsed. For a moment, I can't look away because Amber looks so goddamn *vulnerable* sitting in front of me, her arms clasped tightly in her lap, her ankles entwined in a nervous stance. She knows that I watch her. She knows I watch her sing. *Oh god.* "Singing makes me happy like art makes you happy. Watching me sing...it makes you happy." It's true. *Of course, it's all true.* "So why push that away? Why do you have to be so rude every time I try and get close to you? Why bully me? You want to be my friend. I know you do."

"It doesn't matter," I murmur, surprising myself by the gentleness in my tone. "None of it matters."

Suddenly, I want to cry. I can't talk anymore because she can't hear the way my voice wavers. It's like, there's an ocean inside of me, and it's crashing and pounding relentlessly, and I can't control it. I don't know why it doesn't matter. I don't know why she's so persistent. I don't know what is wrong with me.

"Can I tell you something?" Amber asks tenderly. She kicks her legs off the desk, walks hesitantly over to the bed, and sits next to me.

"I have no doubt you will anyway." I mean it as an insult, but my tone doesn't agree with me. In fact, my tone is shaky and...fond? I sure as hell don't miss the brief smile that flashes across her features when she hears my voice.

"You interest me. Even through all the insults and nicknames...you never could just talk to me like a normal person." She huffs a breath and forces herself to meet my gaze. "I tried to hate you in my lowest moments, when I was crying alone in the bathroom, desperately hoping that I would never see your name on my phone screen ever again—another pathetic comment on my videos. I even thought I'd convinced myself that I *did* hate you. But I didn't, and I can't, and I don't. I want you to be my friend, Ingrid. Sometimes, like now, I think we're getting close to that, but then you go and..."

"Go and *what*?" My voice is harsh. I can't help it. I can feel the walls locking around me, hardening again.

"Ruin it." I'm surprised at her frankness. "I know you want to be my friend, Ingrid." I open my mouth, but Amber cuts me off. "I *know* you do...and that's why." She lets out a sigh, and I can almost see her building up her own walls. "I just want you to be aware of our impending friendship. You can't run from it forever."

I want to say a lot of things. I want to yell. I want to roll my eyes and ask if her need to be friends with a girl who's bullied her for years is some kind of mental disorder. Oddly enough, I want to thank her too. For shattering my walls, for hammering my heart, and for forgiving me.

I want to say so much. But the barricades remain strong.

Amber looks at me with huge eyes and a hesitant smile pressing on her lips. I take one last glance around this room, realising that it is probably the only time I will ever see it. Posters of famous indie bands fill the walls. I stand, feeling Amber's intense gaze on me.

I don't turn around, but I let out a soft "*Okay*," before walking out of the room. I swear that I hear Amber let out a relieved breath behind me.

Chapter Three

SUMMER ISN'T YELLING.

That's what scares me. She watches me carefully, arms crossed comfortably, eyes level. I don't know where Jackson is, but it doesn't matter. Summer matters. My mistake matters. It's my fault, and I need to fix it.

"You were drunk," she begins, huffing out a nervous breath. "You were drunk, but that's no excuse."

I stare around the room, desperate for an escape route. Summer's lectures need to be recorded and sent out to every struggling parent in the country. This isn't the first time I've disappointed her, and I'm sure it won't be the last. I am human. I am flawed. I disappoint people.

"I'm sorry," I gasp. The guilt engulfs me, drying my tongue, prickling my skin. "I wish I could take it back. I messed up."

"You did," she agrees. I hold my breath as her features remain still, her lips pressed tightly together. "You did, but it worked out."

"It was my fault. I should've told him to begin with—or at least told you that I hadn't told him yet."

I dare to crack a grin, and relief floods my bones when she returns it. "I shouldn't have been there in the first place."

"Exactly." She nods. "Although, I think you dug yourself out of that hole by throwing up all over his bedroom floor." Suddenly, she laughs. It's ridiculous and I raise my eyebrows sceptically. She's clutching her stomach, with eyes squeezed tightly shut. It takes a long moment of recovery before they're fluttering open and she is smiling at me. "I'm not mad at you. I wanted to thank you, actually."

"I think you're going a bit far with your forgiveness speech now. Don't get all holy on me."

"No, seriously. I wanted to tell him so badly. I shouldn't have kept it from him, but I was scared. I've made up my mind, but I was scared he'd try to convince me otherwise."

"You've made up your mind?"

"I'm going to keep it." Resolve lingers in her words, and the smile remains, tugging at the corners of her lips. Unconsciously or otherwise, her arms fold protectively against her nonexistent belly. "It's what I want."

"Wow." For a moment, all I can do is consider her braveness in contrast with my cowardly actions. I realise that, for Summer, there were never any other options. "I...I want to help. In any way I can."

Her shoulders sag in what I assume to be a gesture of relief. "I'm glad you say that. You can start by coming with me to my doctor's appointment tomorrow. And be my date to Mum's wedding in June. God knows, I'm going to start getting fat."

I bite my lip. Her requests tell me everything I need to know about Jackson's reaction to her decision. They also tell me that it's not something she wants to talk about right now, so I won't force her.

"Done and done," I confirm. "But seriously, I need to get to art class or they may never let me back. Begging and apologising—that's my theme of the day. I'm on a roll. I need to find Kat and get her to agree to erase last night completely."

Now it's Summer's turn to raise her eyebrows. "You need to tell me what went down last night, Ingrid. And why I saw you leaving school with Amber Freeman."

"She, uh...ugh. Don't worry. I'll tell you later. Do you want me to stay at yours tonight?"

"You better explain later. I don't understand how you went from being so horrible to Amber to following her out of school. How can you make her think that your psycho-bitch moments were nothing but a bit of fun between friends?" I don't miss Summer's sarcasm or the sceptical emphasis she places on *friends*.

"Something like that. Look, I was stupid. It was immature and I was taking my frustration out on her," I admit.

"This wouldn't have anything to do with a recent trip to a gay club, would it?" she breathes. "Ingrid, you know you can tell me anything, right?"

"I know." I press my lips together, avoiding her gaze. "But I have nothing to tell. Really."

"Right." She brushes me off. "That's about as true as me avoiding the fact that I'm currently growing a human inside of me, but, hey, whatever suits you."

MY EYES ARE LOCKED ON the painting in front of me, lips dry. *I didn't mean to...*

It's perfect. The shadow dances from her bare legs. Her brunette curls cascade over her tan shoulders before spilling over her plain white T-shirt. It's an out-of-character white T-shirt that hangs off her perfectly curved shoulders. The oversized shirt fits her perfectly. *So perfectly.* It gapes at the front, showing sculpted collarbones, before falling just over her hips, hinting at a pair of bright pink underwear.

It's blended in with the off-pink background that was lightly shaded as an afterthought, as I attempt to understand what I've just drawn.

Perfect knee-high white socks reach up to the knees of my creation, and the way this portrait stands indicates a stance of comfort—amusement, even.

It's the way those lines have morphed into something more—a picture of meaning, a picture that, in the sickest way of irony, seems to represent my entire high school lie.

I can't breathe. I can't think. I can't consider the painting that has taken over the past three hours of my life. It's perfect. *She's perfect.*

Her eyes are wide, and her lashes graze the skin above her eyelids as she considers me. A coy smile dances on her blush-pink lips. But none of these visual realisations send the spiral of dread plummeting into my stomach until I see *who* I've drawn. The clarity of the drawing, even the feeling it is enticing from me...that is okay. The things I've felt so long but could never express, things that make me want to hide in a corner, never show my face again. The things that made me wish I didn't exist for so long...

I can handle all of that. I can even handle the way that this portrait has luxurious brown hair that topples around her shoulders, held back from her face with only a single pink ribbon.

What I can't handle is the gold *A* that has made itself to the corner of my canvas. I hadn't even thought about it—it was instinct. It was necessary. It said *everything*; everything I feel, everything I am. Everything I am too afraid to be. It represents my worst fears.

Yet, it makes everything perfect.

"Nice drawing," a voice chuckles from behind me.

My body jerks, and I have to resist my first instinct to shove the canvas onto the ground. I whip around to see Kat standing there, her arms crossed loosely over her chest as she nods appraisingly.

"Well, there's that scholarship for RMIT University. We have to do a portrait, so I'm just testing out my abilities," I stammer. "I don't even know if I'm good enough. I've been in this faculty for three years now, and I'm still not getting any better."

"RMIT? Impressive." Kat raises her eyebrows. "And, I dunno, I think you might've found your niche there. You've got some talent. Is that Amber Freeman? I don't even know her, but I'd recognise her from that."

Fuck.

"Yeah, I guess we'd just had a conversation before I got to class, so she's the first person I thought of," I improvise. "Not my best work."

"You should show her." Kat grins, giving me a meaningful look that tells me that she knows *exactly* what she's suggesting. "I think she'd really love it. I've heard she's pretty obsessed with herself. Makes YouTube videos or something? This would be perfect for her."

"I'm just gonna hold on to it," I stammer. "Look, about last night..." I have to change the subject. I have to get away from this painting.

"You were wild. We'll have to do it again sometime."

"Tell that to the guy whose floor I threw up on." I roll my eyes, attempting to ease my hammering heart.

Kat laughs and I immediately feel a little calmer. "No, really, it was fun," she says. "You seemed to be able to let yourself go a little bit. Ever since this whole pink-hair-dye thing, you seem to actually be someone I wouldn't mind hanging out with."

My eyes widen, and I throw everything I can into suppressing my expression. I try not to see the double meaning in her words. Hanging out. That's all. This isn't a gay thing.

"It's amazing what a little hair dye can do, I guess," I answer, feeling a little annoyed. I'm still the same girl, just with pink hair. I haven't changed at all... Have I?

AS I DRIVE Summer to her doctor's appointment, I try not to notice the way she's clutching her hands so tightly in her lap, or the way her whole face is contorting with the effort to keep the calm expression plastered on her face.

"Look, you need to say something because you're stressing me out and I need to not be stressed while I'm driving because you know I'm not a great driver," I blurt out.

"He didn't want to come, Ingrid." Her voice shakes, and I don't need to turn and look at her to see the tears threatening to spill over onto her cheeks. "I told him where and when, and he didn't want to come. He wants nothing to do with this baby."

She cries in earnest now. Her shoulders shake, and pitiful gasps erupt from her lips. I sigh and pull the car over to the side of the road. I switch the engine off and turn to face her.

"Did he tell you that?" I ask abruptly. I have to be abrupt because I know how Summer twists things to make the world seem against her. She makes assumptions and gets offended by literally anything. She is sensitive and kind and strong. But she is so sensitive. And to add hormones on top of that…it's a scary combination.

"No," she splutters. "But he doesn't want to come. He's being so distant from me. This is it now, Ingrid. I know it. I'm going to be a single mother."

I reach over and put a soft hand on her shoulder. She leans into it. "Do you think that maybe he could just be processing things? And maybe he's a little bit hurt that he had to hear the news from drunk me—with a nice side of vomit—rather than you, who found out nearly two weeks ago."

Summer hesitates, and the logic begins to calm her features. "Maybe," she relents.

"I think that's it," I say, turning back to the wheel. "Look, this is my responsibility to get you there safely and on time. So, we need to try and hold back on the mental breakdowns. I'm pretty sure you're about to get your personal space completely violated in the doctor's office, so let's take your mind off that."

"How?" She is still crying a little, but her gasping breaths begin to slow down a little.

"Well…I drew a portrait of Amber yesterday." This is what being a best friend is about. Do I want to admit to this? Absolutely not. Do I want Summer to continue sobbing and thinking about being a single mum? No. So here I am, admitting to this awful thing just to distract her.

"So?"

I raise my eyebrows and avoid turning to face her incredulously as I attempt to concentrate on the road in front of me.

"So, that's *weird*," I say. "Don't you think it's weird?"

"Not really," she answers. "You decided to draw her and you drew her. No big deal. You need to practice your portraits for the RMIT scholarship application, right? I mean, I don't really know why you would decide to draw *her* exactly—I'd be a much better option, if you ask me—but hey, whatever floats your boat."

"I didn't decide to draw her," I admit. "It just kind of happened."

"What? Like an accident?" she scoffs. And then suddenly she is laughing in earnest. "You drew Amber Freeman by accident."

"Summer, this isn't a joke!" I snap, although I am pleased that she's giggling next to me. "She wasn't wearing any pants!"

"Oh god, this just keeps getting better and better," she wheezes, now laughing hysterically. I laugh too as we pull into Summer's doctor's office car park.

Suddenly, my laughter dies in my throat when I see Jackson perched on the benches outside the office. Summer still laughs so hard that she hasn't noticed him yet. I widen my eyes at him and swerve the car around into a car park that faces away from him.

"Summer, I need you to not freak out right now, okay?" I say hesitantly as I put the car into park and let the engine fall quiet.

"I swear to god, Ingrid, if you're about to tell me that you're a lesbian, I'm going to kill you because I called it so long ago." She is still laughing, with fresh tears streaming down her face. Happy tears.

I let out a tired huff. I don't even have the energy to acknowledge her ridiculous comment.

"Jackson is outside."

Summer blanches and immediately whips around her seat, trying to see behind us.

"Jesus, you have a baby inside of you. Can you not attempt to be an acrobat right now?" I mutter. "Look, I'm sure this is his big gesture. He wants you to see that he's okay with this. Maybe I'll just wait here while you two go into the doctor's office?"

The truth is, I don't really know what they do to pregnant ladies at doctor's offices, but I'm pretty sure it involves sticking a huge metal thing where it really shouldn't go, and I would rather not have to witness that.

"He hasn't even told his parents!" Suddenly, Summer's voice is angry. "Jesus, Ingrid, as soon as I saw that second line, I had to tell Mum. How could I not? This isn't *real* for him like it is for me. He's not going to get fat or have to be poked and prodded by doctors, or have to push a freaking baby out of his vagina. He just wants to play happy families without dealing with the reality."

"How do you know that?' I argue. "Summer, you are so damn sensitive sometimes that you think about the worst thing that could happen before you've even had a chance to look for the best in a situation."

"Just come with me." She grips my arm tightly. "*Please*. Even if he is coming around to the idea, I need *you* there. You're my rock."

"And you're mine. Fine, I'll come. But I'm not happy with you—in fact, I resent that lesbian comment."

"You know that I'm right." Summer winks, before quickly throwing the car door open.

I follow suit as she rushes over to Jackson, suddenly interested in what he has to say. As we approach him, he jumps up, smoothing out his out-of-character woollen jumper. I can see his hands shaking from here.

"What are you doing here?" Summer asks coolly.

To my surprise, Jackson turns to me. His eyes are wild and scared. In fact, I've never seen him look so terrified. I shrug. I can't give him all the answers. He should know that by now.

"I'm in this," he says, grabbing Summer's hands.

I step back, feeling extremely awkward, but they don't notice me. They are watching each other. Summer desperately searches his face for truth, for reassurance.

"I want this baby. I want to be a dad, Summer." His voice cracks a little and I suppress a groan. I *really* don't need to be involved in this dramatic moment. "I've told my dad, and he is furious. But I don't care. This is about you. I'm here for you."

Summer nods slightly, but I can still see the cracks of fear threatening to erupt from her calm expression. "Okay. Good. I'm glad you told him. You know that I'm doing this with or without you, but it'll be easier with you."

"Well, it looks like you're free to go then, Ingrid," Jackson says, turning to face me. I frown when I notice the hopeful expression on his face.

Oh. He wants me to leave so he can prove to Summer that he's ready for this.

I suppress the urge to roll my eyes. "Sorry, Jackson, I—"

"She's coming," Summer answers for me. "We're a package deal, and you're just going to have to get used to it."

I grin and follow Summer and Jackson into the doctor's office. It looks like I am well and truly the third wheel. As always.

Summer is quiet in the waiting room, watching the mothers with three sick children or the women with swollen bellies, sitting alone and flipping through magazine. She carefully scrutinises every mother and child, whilst clutching at her own stomach. When her name is called, the blood drains from her face.

Taking the dutiful place of best friend, I take the lead towards the room, with Jackson and Summer trailing behind me. Jesus, do I have to do everything?

When we settle into the comfortable seats of the doctor's office, the doctor—a slightly overweight woman with sandy-blonde hair—turns to me. "My name is Rachel. What can I do for you, Summer?"

"Oh, I'm not Summer; she is." By the betrayed look on Summer's face, I expect that she wished that I would play along and pretend to be her. Although I'm a good friend, I can't be that good.

"I'm pregnant," she blurts out.

Rachel's kind face darkens, and suddenly, I understand why Summer was so scared to speak. "That explains your friends here. Do you need abortion information?"

I gasp, and Summer's face turns to thunder. Jackson sits as still as stone. He appears to be attempting to make his breathing quieter. He looks like he wants to disappear altogether.

"No!" Summer snaps. Already, she is so furious, so protective of this child.

"How old are you, Summer?" the doctor asks. "Seventeen? You really need to consider your options here. Adoption is a great path to take, but there is a social and personal stigma that you need to consider."

I bite down hard on my lip as I brace myself for the explosion of cyclone Summer. I'm prepared for yelling and tears and storming out of this shitty doctor's office—and I'm more than prepared to follow her—but to my complete surprise, she takes a deep breath.

"This is my—*our*—baby," she answers, gripping tightly onto Jackson's leg. His eyes are still wide. "I'm keeping it, and I expected to be treated with respect from you, as my medical practitioner."

I raise my eyebrows, impressed by her calmness. Rachel's face seems to soften too.

"Okay, Summer, that's fine. When was your last period?"

Summer takes another test to confirm the pregnancy, gets her blood pressure and weight checked, and we head into another room to get blood drawn. In fact, I am supremely impressed by the lack of bodily intrusion that Summer has to go through.

After Summer gives blood, we head out into the parking lot. I can see her demeanour is calmer. She is almost floating. The beaming smile that stretched across her face hasn't left since the doctor told her that everything is looking healthy. Jackson is still quiet, pressing his lips together as he watches Summer talk.

"We should go shopping," Summer says excitedly. "I need new clothes and I'm *so* hungry. Let's get food too—lots of food. Mexican!" She chatters excitedly, and I grin at her. I know that things are going to get a lot harder before they get easier, but right now, I let my best friend feel the excitement coursing through her veins.

"Sounds good. Jackson?"

"Yeah, I'm in," he murmurs, snaking his hand around Summer's waist. "I'll follow along in my car. Shall we go to that Mexican place in the mall? That way you can go shopping afterwards, if you like."

Summer's musical laugh tells me that the plan is perfect.

Chapter Four

IT'S ACTUALLY JACKSON who pulls Summer in the direction of a baby shop. I know it's way too early for her to be thinking about buying anything, but suddenly, they are wandering inside, and I am walking through the mall alone.

I never liked window-shopping; actually, I never liked shopping in general. Those shop lights and skinny mannequins make me look at my huge thighs—and they *are* huge. From years of emotional eating and then running in my older years, they are strong and big. My body is curved, and sometimes, it feels like there are curves in all of the wrong places. I have huge hips and a small bust. I can never find clothes that fit in all of the right places. Not like Summer can.

"If that's where you want to shop, then you're looking in all the wrong places." A voice makes its way through the white noise of the mall, and I turn around, curious.

Of course.

Kat stands a few metres behind me, hands on her hips and grinning wildly. I laugh a little and walk towards her, shaking my head.

"You really need to stop sneaking up on me," I say.

Her grin grows, if possible, even wider. "Sneaking up on you would be telling you that I saw you standing outside the baby shop, talking very seriously to some people. You're not knocked up, are you, Pinkie? Because that would ruin *all* of my fun."

I ignore the way my breath seems to catch at the back of my throat, and the way that Kat's eyes are locked on me meaningfully. Again, my mouth is dry and my chest feels tight. Jesus, why does this girl always need to make things so awkward?

"No," I stammer. "I was just saying goodbye to my friends."

"Oh, so *she's* pregnant?" Kat raises a curious eyebrow.

I sigh. She seems to share my love for gossip. Too bad that this piece of gossip is never going to escape my lips again—blurting it out to Jackson was enough for one lifetime.

"Nope. I don't know why you think that. We were just standing in front of a random shop."

"Let's get coffee," she insists.

I shrug, just thankful to have escaped *that* particularly awkward conversation. We head into one of the chain coffee shops—the coffee is terrible, but I'm a sucker for those big comfortable lounge chairs that line the windows. We order our coffees and collapse into the comfortable chairs. The silence settles over us.

I've never been the most sociable of people. I like to be alone and comfortable. But the silence that settles between us is surprisingly comfortable, and a smile twitches at the corner of Kat's lips.

"You know, I have never seen someone change so much as you have in the past two weeks."

"You don't even know me!" I snort. "Jesus, you're acting like you've done a PhD study on me or something."

"I like to watch people. Just like you do. And you have changed."

"No, I haven't," I argue. Why am I arguing? She's probably right.

"You're getting more comfortable in your sexuality. I bet it's that damn hair. It's given you a more confident personality."

"Bullshit. I'm still the same person. The only difference is that you've actually put an effort into getting to know me, rather than treating me like a piece of decrepit furniture behind the gymnasium."

"You're letting me get to know you," she retorts. "Think about it. Would you ever have accepted an invitation to a *gay club* last year?"

"To be fair, I didn't know it was a gay club until I got there."

"But you didn't leave."

"You're right, I didn't leave," I echo.

Maybe she's right. I don't know how or why. Maybe she's just stoned. But her words are resonating inside of me, and I'm thinking about my painting of Amber. Suddenly, I have the overwhelming, incredible urge to get so drunk that I forget my own name.

The flamboyant barista brings our coffees over, and I take a sip, ignoring the scalding, bitter coffee that burns my throat. I just need something to do with my hands because, right now, Kat is scrutinising me.

"Are you gay, Ingrid?"

"No."

She pauses to take a sip of her own coffee—I can smell the sickly-sweet scent of hazelnut from across the table.

"Okay." I expect to see a sceptical expression coat her features, like Jackson and Summer, but instead she just shrugs. "That's fine."

"Can we go out again?" I ask. "Soon. The club was fun."

"Why was it so fun?" Kat fires back, raising an eyebrow.

"I don't know," I say, staring down at my latte as if it holds the answers. "I liked the dancing. And the drinking."

"Did you like grinding on me?" she asks.

I nearly choke on my coffee, and it sloshes out over the sides of the cup, coating my hands in sticky, hot liquid.

"I was drunk. I just want to get drunk and having a good time, okay? You need to stop making this to be something that it isn't."

She doesn't recoil from my sharp tone like I expect her to. We really don't know each other well enough for me to be so abrupt with her, but I can't help it. The anger and frustration boils over before I can help it.

"The club is having a themed night on Friday," she says, ignoring my angry words.

"What's the theme?"

"Fancy dress." She grins, as if it's some kind of conspiracy. "Obviously, you haven't seen how the gays do fancy dress, but it's something you don't want to miss."

"Are *you* gay?" I ask, before I can stop myself. It feels so intrusive to ask her that, and I feel like I have no right to know. So why is everyone asking me?

"I don't know. I think I'm just experimenting. I do what I want. Mostly I'm into girls. Although, sometimes when I'm drunk, nothing beats a good, strong man, if you know what I mean."

I give her an absent smile, wishing that I *did* actually know what she meant. "So, what do I have to dress up as?"

"Anything you can dream of, my friend. I take it that you're coming, then?"

"Well, it sounds like this is something I wouldn't want to miss," I answer. "And besides, I need to be drunk."

"Why?" she asks.

I shake my head. "I don't even know the answer to that, so you can't expect me to give you one."

"Okay," she says, turning back to her coffee—if that sweet concoction can even be called coffee. "That's fine."

I am thinking about her answer to my question. *I'm just experimenting...* She was so calm, so sure. How can she be so comfortable with saying that? Why can't I even think about that? *Experimenting.* Isn't that what we all do, as humans? We experiment. We make mistakes. We figure out where we are meant to be.

"Maybe I should do that," I murmur.

"What?"

"Experiment." I mumble the words into my coffee, feeling the scorch begin to simmer across my cheeks. *God,* why did I say that? What is wrong with me?

Kat is silent for a long moment. So long that I let my mortified gaze drift back to her. She is watching me with a curious expression twisting on her lips. "If that's what you want to do, Pinkie..." For the first time since I met her, I can see Kat holding something back. There is something that she wants to say, dancing on the edge of her lips, but she's pressing them together tightly, regarding me with that careful expression. Her maroon lipstick gives her a touch of darkness.

I don't push her. I don't even know if I want to hear what she has to say. I don't even know what I'm saying anymore. I feel like I'm going crazy.

"You're not going crazy, if that's what you're worried about," Kat tells me reassuringly, as if she's reading my thoughts. "I've been you. Both versions of you. Just take things slowly and see what happens. Stop overthinking things."

I almost laugh aloud, but I can see the genuine reassurance coming from her green eyes. She really is trying to help me.

But I don't need help...do I?

"Look, I should probably go and find my friends," I say, quickly downing the rest of my coffee, relishing the way that the bitterness radiates through my body. It numbs everything else. I want to be numb.

"I thought you were saying goodbye to them." She lets out a gruff laugh. "I'm messing with you. Go and find them. Don't worry, I won't tell anyone where they went."

"They didn't *go* anywhere..." I mumble. There is no point trying to reason with Kat. She's already caught on. Oddly, I trust that she won't tell anyone. Of course, Summer won't be able to hide the truth forever, but she will be in control when it comes out. This is her secret; this is her reality. I will support her for as long as I need to. "Thanks for the chat."

Again, Kat shrugs, leisurely sipping on her drink. "You needed it. I'll see you Friday?"

"Definitely." I nod, relishing in the thought that in two days, I will be free to get as drunk as I need to. I'm excited for a good night.

"See you, Pinkie."

"Bye," I say, turning away.

I can feel Kat's gaze following as I exit the coffee shop, and I'm aware of every move I make. I turn to wander through the mall, knowing that Jackson and Summer are probably nowhere near finished their make-believe fun in the baby shop. I don't want to intrude—I want to let them look at the tiny socks and cute toys for a little longer and forget about the grim reality of being teen parents.

And so, I walk through the strip of stores, trying to ignore the thoughts that are pounding through my mind, avoiding the reality of everything that is encompassing me, stopping me from acknowledging everything that I want to be, all of the history and repression that are holding me back.

Couples walk by hand in hand, nuzzling into each other's shoulders, laughing at a joke that only they understand. Mothers with babies strapped to their chest coo at their child, while supportive fathers rub their spouses' backs. Happy people, smiling people, carefree people. I wonder why I can't be like them. Why can't I have what they have? Am I not capable of being like them?

Absent-mindedly, I find myself walking towards the only adult costume shop in our little town. Since it's known for its raunchy costumes and crazy outfits, I'm hoping that I can find something that will be good enough for this crazy night that Kat has planned.

"Ingrid? What are you doing here?"

I whip around because that voice resonates with me. It's the voice that has the capability of sending chills dancing down my spine, the voice that has lilted through my headphones as I listen to it sing...

Amber stands in the doorway of the bookshop next door, grinning at me. I step away from the costume shop, shoving my hands sheepishly into my jeans so that she can't see them shaking.

"Oh, it's you." My voice is an unexcited monotonic drone. "Hey."

She presses her lips together, and her eyes glint as she fights back laughter. Today, her hair is piled in a messy bun on top of her head, with wisps of mahogany strands falling onto her face. She's wearing makeup, which both surprises and enthrals me. Bright-red lipstick adorns her full lips, and her mascara-laden lashes dance along her cheekbones.

"You need a costume?" she asks quizzically. "What for?"

I curse myself for her curiosity. God damn, why does this girl need to know everything?

"Just a party. Why do you care?"

"I could use a good party." She grins, ignoring my sharp tone. "Exam season is killing me."

My heart is *already* hammering. What the hell is wrong with me? I stare at her, trying my best to make the stare more intimidating than admiring.

"I don't think you'd be interested in this party," I improvise. "Besides, you'd have to hang out with me, and we both know that isn't anyone's idea of fun."

This time, she does laugh. It's a musical laugh—but of course, everything that Amber Freeman does is musical.

"And we both know that's not true." I can't read her tone and that is killing me. Can she see how tense my body is right now? I lean against the door frame of the bookstore, attempting to mask my nerves. "Come on. Where's this party? I think it could be fun—we are friends now, after all."

I fight every defence I have that comes bubbling to the surface. Every snide remark or hurtful comment dies in my throat, falling into the pits of my stomach, making me feel sick with their weight.

I want to fight it. I want to fight *her*. I hate this. I hate her.

I hate myself.

"It's at Cloud Nine," I blurt out. My voice is shaking now. "I guess you've probably never heard of it." I'm banking on the fact that she's never heard of it. I hope she's never heard of it.

Please never have heard of it.

"Of course, I've heard of it! You don't try to launch a career in singing without knowing about the town's only gay club. You obviously don't know much about the music industry." Her tone is playful, and I fight with everything I have the smile that's jumping at the corners of my lips, but it's spreading over my face faster than I can stop it. "I didn't peg you to be the kind of girl to hang out at lesbian clubs. I didn't even think you had a fake ID."

"You don't really know me though, do you?" I ask.

"I think I do, Ingrid."

Suddenly, everything in this mall seems far less interesting than the expression on Amber's face. The screaming children, laughing couples, ridiculous pop music that blasts over the radio all fades away, and Amber is right in front of me, smiling kindly.

I don't have a defence anymore. I'm waiting for that ice-cold stance to fall over me, with cruel words and sharp tones, a strong glare and a cool attitude, but it's gone. I've lost it.

And Amber is standing there, watching me expectantly.

"I guess you can come if you want. The girl I'm going with—Kat—is pretty cool."

My mind is spinning as the words escape my uncooperative lips. She *can't* come.

"Just give me a time and date and I'll be there." She grins, studying my expression. "You do *want* me to come, right? I mean, I'm not intruding on anything...like a date?"

I lift my eyebrows. Is she asking if I'm dating *Kat*? The words are tumbling from my lips before I can stop them, awkwardly dancing around the subject as I attempt to save myself from this encounter. The words are jumbled and my tone is all wrong. I am messing this up *so* badly.

"Yeah, you can come. It's fine. You'll just have to find a costume and meet us there. I'm sure it will be fun, and if it's not, that's what alcohol is for."

She laughs as I ramble, attempting to make it seem casual. If it's so casual, why is my heart hammering? Why do my clothes feel too small and my face far too hot? Why is Amber smiling at me like she knows a secret? Why are her eyes glowing at me with this intensity that I can't seem to escape?

"I guess it is." She shrugs nonchalantly. "Okay, good luck finding a costume. I'll see you there. I'm looking forward to it."

I blanch, make an awkward sound caught between a cough and a laugh, and rush into the costume shop without saying another word.

What is wrong with me?

As I browse through the ridiculously sexualised costumes, I analyse every moment of my conversation with Amber. Why can't I talk to her like a normal person? Why have I turned from an ice-cold bitch to a fumbling, awkward mess? There is no such thing as a normal conversation when it comes to Amber. What if I really am in love with her or something?

It's that thought that sends my shaking limbs into shuddering sobs, and I'm standing in the corner of the costume shop crying quietly. My hands grip onto a fairy costume as the tears drip onto my cheeks. My breath is gasping, and snot threatens to make an appearance.

I'm such a mess.

So, as I stand in the corner of the costume shop, gripping the fairy costume as if it holds my life answers and crying quietly, I make a decision to stop worrying. This is killing me—Kat said it all. I overthink everything, I worry too much. I make a big deal out of things when I don't have to. I am torturing myself.

I wipe my sleeve over my face, sniffling as I attempt to control my breathing. I am not in love with Amber. I am not in love with anyone. I'm awkward around her because for some reason, I used to be a bully. An utter bitch. Maybe it's my only-child syndrome. Maybe I'm just a bad person. My history of bullying her embarrasses me. We were young, and I was stupid. I would leave rude comments on her videos; I would make bitchy comments about her. I couldn't be controlled.

As I consider the reasons why Amber is getting to me, I take a heavy breath. All I have to do is get ridiculously drunk at this costume party and everything will be okay.

I buy the overpriced fairy costume without even trying it on. I need to get back to Summer and Jackson. I need some kind of sanity in my life right now.

With a jolt, I realise how bad things must be if I'm thinking that Summer and Jackson are the epitome of sanity.

Chapter Five

I REREAD THE scholarship guidelines, twining my hands in my lap nervously. *I'm not good enough.* That's my first thought as I scroll through the requirements—which I barely pass. *I don't deserve it.* That's my second thought as I read through the suggested art demonstrations that the application requires.

I don't even know how to boil an egg. How am I supposed to move away from home and attend this huge university in less than a year? There are people who live art, who breathe pencil lines and watercolours...people who have won awards, who have demonstrated excellence all through high school. *I am not good enough.*

I think about my accidental portrait. It feels so wrong and invasive. I shouldn't have ever even thought about drawing her. *But I didn't think...* It was instinct. And then there is that tiny, weak voice in the back of my mind telling me that the portrait is *good.* It could get me the scholarship I need to make it into RMIT.

I should've tried harder, made more of an effort in the last three years. I should've applied for the out-of-school clubs or made an effort with the community shows that always seemed so lame. Maybe participated in the competitions or awards that our school always seemed to have. I did nothing. I was so lazy.

My eyes are trained on my computer screen, at the RMIT application, and wonder what else I have in my life. Do I have any other plans? Do I have any other dreams? I want to draw. I want to paint. I want to create beauty.

This is it. This is all I've got.

I pull out my sketchbook, stained with coffee rings and full of crumbs of food. There are torn pages, scribbles everywhere, and messy ideas scrawled underneath doodles of majestic mountain scenes and curvaceous bodies embracing each other.

I flick through the eyes and lips and hairstyles that have distracted me, elephants and bears cover my pages...watercolour, pencil, paint, even pen. I used any tool I could to create whatever was growing inside of me. The ideas that poured onto the pages, stained with tears and memories and pain and growth. I need to be good enough. This is something that I can't procrastinate or avoid or pull out of. I need to put myself out there. I need to try.

And it's so terrifying, so scary, because putting myself out there means I could be rejected. It means *I* might not be good enough.

I snap my laptop shut and throw my sketchbook onto the bed. The negativity is pouring into me, and I need to avoid it, so I call the one person who can brutally make me snap out of it without actually breaking my soul.

SUMMER IS SHOVELLING nachos into her mouth like she hasn't eaten for weeks. She isn't even listening anymore. I can just see her glancing around the restaurant, as if silently willing a waitress to come by so she can order more guac.

I down the rest of my drink attempting to calm my annoyance. I can't be mad because this is who Summer is—pregnant or not. The girl likes food more than meaningful conversation, and I can't say that I blame her.

"I can't believe you invited Amber to a lesbian club," she snorts into her nachos. "Seriously, Ingrid, you're not doing anything for those gay rumours."

"She basically invited herself. She has no friends. She's probably desperate for something to do that doesn't involve making pathetic YouTube videos on a Friday night."

"Jackson told me you watch her videos, you know," Summer says bluntly, finally turning away from her nachos. "Look, I don't know why you didn't tell me, and I'm not mad at you, but you really need to take a good, hard look at things. Because, right now, you're not making sense. You are a total bitch to her, but you know her uploading schedule. You are so awkward around her. Are you into her or not? If you think anyone is going to judge you, then you really are overthinking everything. The only person who cares about your sexuality is you, Ingrid."

I lean back into the booth chair, stung by her sharp tone. For once, I am not appreciative of Summer's bluntness. Maybe it's the fact that she spent every second at school today with Jackson or the fact that this is the first time in a week that she's been able to speak about something other than her pregnancy, but I'm starting to wonder if she was the wrong person to call.

Maybe I should've called Kat.

"I didn't call you to talk about this," I respond coolly. "Actually, I need your advice about this RMIT scholarship."

"Well, you *have* to apply," Summer says, as if it's the most obvious thing in the world. "I've seen your art. You've got talent."

"But what if I don't?" I ask, finally letting the fear cascade into my words. "I don't know any of that technical stuff. I never even really paid attention in art class until I was allowed to go off and do my own thing. I don't know about theory and structure or what is right or wrong. The last three years, I've just been winging it. I make it up as I go along."

"*Exactly*," Summer says, pausing to take another few bites of her nachos. "You are already so good, even though you're lazy as hell. Imagine how great you'd be if you actually put some effort into it? Learnt some theory and did some of those ridiculous exercises or whatever it is you do in art class? You need to apply for this scholarship, and you're going to get in. And I'm just going to have to come and live with you while I'm covered in shit and puke with a baby attached to me constantly because I'm not going to stay here while you go off and do amazing things."

I smile at my best friend as she absent-mindedly rests her hands on her nonexistent stomach. "Well, thanks. You know what to say to make me feel better."

"I'm not saying this to make you feel better!" she argues. "This is the truth. You are good enough. You just need to apply yourself and put a little more effort into things."

"And now you sound like my mum." I roll my eyes.

She grins. "Good! I've been practising my mum voice. I know that I've always been good at lecturing people, but I really needed to work on that condescending tone our parents use to make us feel like shit."

I laugh loudly. "Well, consider that skill perfected."

"Now I just have to work on being able to clean up someone else's shit without vomiting on them."

"Yeah, I don't think your baby—or Jackson—would appreciate it if that happened," I say. "I'm sorry for being so weird about Amber. I don't know what's wrong with me."

"There's nothing *wrong* with you," she murmurs. "You're just trying to figure out your place in life. You just need to start being honest with yourself. You don't even need to be honest with me, if you don't want to." She gives me a look that says she won't be happy about this at all. "If you want to go to a gay club with Amber, go for it. But I'm going to call a duck a duck and say that there might be a little more to this ridiculous friendship than you're willing to admit."

She watches me carefully, and I remain still as I digest her words. She's right. Of course, she's always right. But I can't force anything—I don't *know* how I feel. I don't know what's wrong with me.

"So, am I imagining things, or did I see Jackson's name on the arts list this afternoon?" I change the subject in one sweeping sentence. "Because he really is leaving it a little too late. He's not applying for the RMIT scholarship, is he?"

Summer shrugs. "You'll have to ask him. Right now, all we're talking about is what's in my stomach. If he wants to do art, I guess I'm going to support him. It's what he wants to do."

I don't bother telling Summer that I've known that since our early high school days. I'm curious as to why this is suddenly so important to Jackson. Maybe he's starting to realise that he's spent the last three years trying to make everyone else happy and abandoned the one thing that makes him happy.

Or is that me who's doing that?

"How are his parents taking this pregnancy news?" I ask curiously.

Summer tenses up and sits a little straighter, pushing her nachos away as if they suddenly disgust her. "His dad...actually, uh, they kicked him out."

"Shit," I breathe.

"Yeah" She frowns. "And my mum isn't going to let him stay with us for much longer. I mean, she knows that we can't get in any more trouble since I'm already pregnant, but she says he's lazy and eats too much food. You know how she is."

Summer's mother is a clean freak, to put it mildly. In fact, I can't ever imagine Jackson setting foot in Summer's house, let alone living there. He is the opposite of clean—typical boy.

"Where is he going to go?" I ask.

"I don't know." Suddenly Summer's voice cracks and there are tears filling her blue eyes, and she is more emotional than I've seen her in a while. "Damn pregnancy hormones," she mutters. "It's just frustrating because we *should* be living together. We should have our own home and little dog, and there should be a ring on my finger."

"Oh, Summer." I sigh as she composes herself, delicately tapping away the tears from under her eyes. "You've always been the kind of girl to do things out of order. Who wants to follow boring tradition anyway? You guys will get all of that, but right now, you're trying to figure things out. Just like I am."

"I guess. I'm just worried. What if we can't make it work?"

I know what she's saying. Her mother is getting married for the third time. Summer has had to go through the heartbreak, the excitement, the fear...the whole cycle. She's watched her mum be used and let down time after time, and now she's just hoping that husband-number-three is here to stay. That's not what she wants for her own child.

"You will," I tell her confidently. "But that's way too much for anyone to think about—let alone a hormonal pregnant lady. So, right now, we're going to order some dessert and figure out what to do about problem-number-one. We need to find Jackson a place to live."

"I CAN'T BELIEVE she told you," Jackson huffs, throwing his sketchbook down onto the table dramatically. "I'm sorry, but it's none of your business."

"Hey, chill with the attitude," I say. Thankfully, we have the art room to ourselves on this early Friday morning. It looks like all of the art students are too lazy to come to class—or too busy preparing for the party at Cloud Nine tonight. The butterflies in my stomach are violent as I think about that. "Why are you being so cold all of a sudden?"

Jackson looks down at the desk sheepishly, twirling his pencil between his fingers. "I'm just stressed. I should never have changed to arts. I should be looking for a full-time job."

"Oh, Jacks." I sigh. "This is what you want to do. I'm glad you stood up to your dad. You should've done it years ago."

He laughs abruptly. "You know, this is why he kicked me out. Not the pregnancy thing."

"Bullshit."

"I'm serious," he says, eyes wide. "He was angrier about me joining the art faculty than about Summer being pregnant. It's pathetic."

"You should be glad he kicked you out. What a dick," I huff. "I'm happy you're doing art. Your comics are good! You've got talent."

"So do you. You were probably my biggest motivation, actually. I saw you painting one afternoon when I came to look around. You had your headphones in and didn't even notice me, but as soon as I saw what you were painting, I thought, *Wow, I want to do something like that.* I want to create."

"I'm glad I inspired you." I grin. "I've been told that I'm quite the inspiration."

"But also, it's kind of your fault I'm homeless now, so..." Jackson's voice is playful and his eyes sparkled with the joke, but I can't help the sting of guilt that shoots through me with his words.

"Maybe you should just stay with me then if staying with Summer gets too intense," I say. "I know my mum would be cool with it."

Jackson looks hopeful. "What about Summer?"

"What about her?" I ask.

"Don't you think...it's kind of weird? I remember what we used to get up to in that bedroom of yours," he says pointedly.

"Those days are over, and Summer never needs to know," I blush. "As far as I'm concerned, it never happened. It's like cousins learning to kiss. No big deal."

"Kissing cousins?" Jackson laughs, letting his pencil fall onto the desk with a clatter. "You really are all sorts of fucked up, Ingrid."

I snort, turning back to my sketchbook. "Look, you are fathering my best friend's child and I'm going to a gay club with Amber Freeman tonight. I don't think either of us needs to worry about the boundaries if you lived with me."

Jackson is silent for a moment, studying me carefully. "If by boundaries, you mean no more playing with yourself while you watch Amber's videos, then I'm all for it." His joke falls flat, and the uncomfortable silence settles between us. "And...did you just say what I think you said...?"

"Yes," I snap. "Now, shut up before I change my mind and make you homeless again."

I EXAMINE MYSELF in the mirror, fidgeting with the scratchy fabric of this ridiculously short green fairy dress. The dress strains tightly over my hips before flowing out above my thighs. The neckline is ridiculously low, revealing my almost nonexistent cleavage. I readjust my bra, attempting to give myself a boost.

The fishnet stockings give a mysterious air to the ridiculous fairy costume. I have paired them with bulky biker boots. I am a bad fairy.

My makeup is dark, to match the boots. I have maroon lipstick and silver sparkles around my eyes. I practise my evil-fairy expression in the mirror.

I look ridiculous.

But my pink hair looks great with the outfit, giving it the perfect touch of playful innocence. If fairies existed, I'm sure they'd be laughing at me.

As I gather my necessities for the night—Kat has even equipped me with a decent fake ID—I wonder about Amber. This is the first time that I've let myself think about the possibilities that tonight may hold.

Before I know it, my feet take me to the kitchen and I grab the bottle of cheap wine from the fridge. What is it that they say? Liquid confidence? Either way, I'm going to need to be drunk before the night even starts if I'm going to survive this.

I'm stumbling by the time I meet Kat outside Cloud Nine. The world spins, and I realise that drinking an entire bottle of wine on the bus ride here probably wasn't the greatest idea. Kat is with a tall, dark guy. *Is he real, or am I just imagining him?*

"Hey," I slur, blinking rapidly. "There are two of you, right?"

"Jesus." Kat snorts. "You need to sober the fuck up, or they aren't going to let you in, Pinkie. Why the pre-drinks? You know we can make our own fun." The guy beside her snorts and snaps into focus a little. His huge brown eyes gaze down at me, his full lips curling up in amusement. "This is Leon. He needs a distraction tonight."

"Ex-girlfriend problems," he explains.

"What're you meant to be dressed as?" I question him, watching him intently. Kat's costume is obvious, and I shouldn't have expected anything different. Her black police leotard has been cut to show side-boob *as well* as under-boob. Kat knows how to dress up. Her streaky blue hair is tied into a tight bun on top of her head, with a black police hat to match. Her thigh-high boots are the only thing covering her legs.

Outrageous is an understatement.

"Jesus, she's too drunk to even read your shirt." Kat giggles as she places a heavy hand on my shoulder. "Come on, sit down. We're going to get you a smoke while we wait for your friend."

I collapse onto the pavement, squinting at Leon's shirt. I make out blurry words written in what seems to be permanent marker that say *This Is My Costume.* The white of his shirt contrasts with his black skin, and in my feeble state, I feel as if I need to squint just to look at him.

Kat lights up something that definitely isn't just tobacco, and I take it from her. I need something, *anything.* I'm not numb enough.

Where is Amber?

I smoke slowly, letting it spill into my mind and numb my body. Kat and Leon watch me, amused. I don't even give it back to her, I just keep smoking. It is keeping me alive and calming me down. This is what I need right now.

"Bets on puke time?" Leon asks. I feel a heavy hand resting on my bare thigh, and I look down, curiously. His hands are *huge* and...warm. I lean into him, feeling a hard shoulder protectively pushing against me. Black curls cover his forehead and dance in front of his eyes. He doesn't seem bothered by them.

"I think you should be putting bets on bang time." Kat giggles. "She's into you."

"Fuck that," Leon says. "She's trashed."

"The night is young, my friend." I grin.

He laughs uncomfortably, wrapping a hand around my waist. "Keep smoking," he murmurs. "It'll help."

I'm starting to wonder what is actually in this cigarette and if it has magical powers, when I see Amber approaching. I drop the cigarette, coughing loudly. I'm still spluttering as Leon dives down to rescue the smoke and Kat breaks into a fit of giggles.

I never expected to see Amber strutting towards us in a typical slutty cat costume. *What?!* The leotard is cut low to show off her ample cleavage. The only other thing she wears is cat ears and a pair of stiletto black heels. No tights, no bra.

My mouth is suddenly very dry and I don't know if it's the smoke or Amber, but if I'm honest with myself, it's probably Amber.

It's definitely Amber.

"Can we go inside? It's freezing," she says in way of greeting. "Jesus, is she already drunk?"

Amber's perturbed question seems to break through my sluggish thoughts. I can't control my giddy smirk, as I let my gaze roam across her extreme outfit.

"I'm not drunk anymore." I grin. *I'm definitely still drunk.* "The pot fixed it."

Leon laughs and pulls me into a standing position. Kat introduces herself to Amber with a flirty smile dancing across her lips. I lean into Leon, taking slow breaths. People always accuse me of being a lightweight when it comes to alcohol, and I'm starting to understand their annoyances, but smoking seems to have helped.

"Hey." Amber breaks away from her conversation with Kat to talk to me. "Let's go and have some fun."

And so, our odd little group walks—or in my case, stumbles—into Cloud Nine.

The bouncer doesn't give me a second glance as we are ushered into the club. The thumping music and smell of sex and alcohol assaults my senses. I widen my eyes as I attempt to take in the scene that greets me in my drunken state. If I thought my last experience at Cloud Nine was crazy, I have no idea what I was expecting tonight.

I see girls whose faces have become full tigers—with real whiskers poking from their cheeks, girls who wear scrubs and masks, girls wearing nothing but tassels on their nipples and a nude G-string. Girls, girls, girls. Everywhere.

Beside me, I hear Amber gasp. "Well, I don't feel so underdressed now," she mutters, but the appreciation shines through her words. She's impressed.

"Let's dance!" I shout over the thumping music, meeting Amber's eyes and grinning widely. The awkwardness is shattered in the overwhelming atmosphere. Suddenly, the silence isn't scary and my mouth isn't dry anymore.

"Drinks first!" Amber laughs in response.

Chapter Six

LEON'S ERECTION GRINDS into the tulle of my fairy skirt. His hands grip my waist so tightly that I'm sure there will be bruises in the morning. I shake my hips as we sway with the music, letting my lips caress his sweaty neck. The alcohol is thumping through my body, and all I can see are blurry bodies, embracing each other, dancing with each other, loving each other.

My hands clasp Leon's ass as he pushes himself closer towards me, thrusting along with the music. Beside us, Kat and Amber dance together, laughing loudly as they drunkenly throw their arms into the air. I don't even notice the other people around us. I can only see my friends.

My skin is buzzing and my blood is pulsing, I let my urges control me as I pull myself closer to Leon, so close that our faces touch. He breathes hard as he locks gazes with me, groping my waist and trailing his hands down farther. His huge brown eyes are so wide as he stares at me, his tongue flicking over his full lips.

"You're so beautiful," he gasps.

Kat watches us. I break my gaze with him to look at her and Amber. They're openly staring at us as we dance. Kat looks impressed and Amber looks confused. I turn back to Leon, too drunk to care about what anyone thinks of me. He smiles at me, pressing his forehead against mine. Suddenly, our lips touch and his tongue slips into my mouth. He moans and pushes his body closer to mine, pulling me tighter, kissing me harder.

The music thumps through my body, replacing the alcohol, sending me further into the spirals of bliss in this pounding room. I am a part of something bigger. These flashing lights, these pounding bodies, the alcohol that bubbles through me, the boy that I am kissing...it's a part of something bigger. I want to let go.

I pull away from him, mumbling something about more alcohol as I stumble towards the bar. He lets me go after giving my shoulder one last squeeze. I have one goal in mind—to be drunker. I push my way through the mess of bodies, determined to get to the bar. Finally, TJ meets my eyes and grins as he pours my drink.

"Ingrid, Ingrid! Me too! Me too!"

I whirl around to see Amber stumbling towards me, looking almost as drunk as I feel. She waves her hands at us, and TJ laughs.

"I dunno if she should be havin' anymore." He grins.

"Oh, she can handle it." I shouldn't trust my lips to speak right now because I can't judge Amber's ability to handle another drink, but there's a seductive voice whispering in my ear, telling me that she should have another drink.

We should both have another drink.

Suddenly, Amber presses her body against mine and encircles my waist with her arms as she sloppily leans into my neck. "I saw you makin' out with Leon," she slurs into my shoulder. "Rude."

TJ slides two brightly coloured cocktails across the bar, paired with two dark shots. He smiles knowingly, throwing me a wink. "Drink up, ladies!"

I pass Amber the shot, and we drink it quickly, laughing as we scrunch up our faces. The alcohol tingles through me, numbing me further, making me feel alive. I am exhilarated. I am numb. I am happy.

Amber's body is so close to mine. She studies the cocktail carefully before drinking it in a single gulp. The dark makeup on her eyes hypnotises me. I can't look away. She looks stunning.

I want to kiss her.

The thought hits me like a slap in the face, and I slam it down with the rest of my drink, tearing my body away from Amber's warm hands. I don't miss the flash of hurt that strikes across her face.

"Let's dance," I mutter.

I can see Leon watching me from the dance floor, a flirty smile dancing on his lips as he meets my eyes. I walk straight towards him, abandoning Amber in the sea of dancing bodies. I can't be near her right now. I can't be near her *ever*.

Leon grabs me by the waist, kissing my neck. "Come back to my house," he breathes in my ear.

I push my body farther into him, letting my hips thrust against his with the beat of the music. I need to get away from Amber, as far away as possible. I need to be near Leon.

"Okay," I murmur.

Kat and Amber have disappeared, and suddenly, Leon and I are alone, dancing in the middle of crazy costumes and crazy people. The music has reached a deafening pitch, and it vibrates through my body. I let it engulf me and wash away every fear and worry. I don't need to think about Amber right now. I don't need to think about *anything* right now.

This music, this alcohol, this boy. It's everything I need.

"SO, DID YOU bang him?" Summer grins, shovelling the syrup-laden pancakes into her mouth.

I groan and turn my attention back to the pancakes in front of me. The smell of coffee and sweet pastries in this little café is overwhelming but welcoming to my hung-over stomach.

"Obviously. Look, if you'd seen him, you'd understand." I try to ignore the sceptical expression that flicks across Summer's features. I don't need her judgement, not when I can barely comprehend what happened last night myself.

"Ingrid, I think even if he was the next cover model for Calvin Klein, I still wouldn't understand," Summer scoffs, sipping her hot chocolate as she eyes my coffee with envy. Apparently, she's still adjusting to the news that you can't have too much caffeine whilst pregnant.

"Look, I would rather talk about literally anything else right now. Even if it's your hairy pregnant nipples. I am too hung-over to think about anything to do with alcohol or my craziness last night."

"Amber?" Summer grins, winking at me. She seems to notice my distraught expression and quickly changes the subject. "My mum's wedding."

"Your mum's wedding?" I raise an eyebrow.

"You're still going to be my date, right?" Summer bites her lip. "Look, I have enough trouble dealing with Satan himself. I don't need to worry about this wedding."

"Wait, Satan himself? Are you talking about Jackson or Mark?" I ask, referring to her soon-to-be stepdad.

"Mark." She rolls her eyes. "Jackson has been demoted to pesky demon, since he's been so good lately."

"Then why can't you go to the wedding with Jackson? The demon and Satan? I'm sure they could get along." I don't want to tell Summer that I don't know if I can deal with her family politics right now, not when I'm going through my own mental crisis.

"Mark *hates* Jackson. And even more now that I'm pregnant. Of course, he hates me too, so that makes sense. Look, you're my security blanket. I need to be there for my mum and you need to be there for me. I'm getting fatter and fatter every day. I need you to help me find a dress and walk me down the aisle." She winks at me.

I can see the genuine concern under Summer's joking smirk. I'm her best friend and I need to be there for her. Sometimes, being a friend means shoving my internal crisis to the side to deal with her internal crisis.

"Of course. I'm used to finding dresses to fit *my* fat body, so I'm sure I can help you out. I don't have the excuse of being pregnant, though."

Summer rolls her eyes. "Call yourself fat again and I'll be eating the rest of your pancakes as a punishment. Thank you, though. It means a lot."

I throw my attention back to my pancakes, because my stomach growls at the reminder. "Last night was crazy." I don't know why the words escape my lips, but it's coming back in flashes now.

"Where did Amber end up?" Summer knows where I ended up because she picked me up from Leon's house this morning.

"I have no idea," I answer truthfully. Of course, I don't add what else is on my mind—that I'd very much like to know where Amber ended up. Did she go home with Kat? Did anything happen between them? Why do I even care?

"Did, uh, did anything happen?" Summer asks carefully, studying the food in front of her.

I ignore the stabs of annoyance that bolt through me. I bring this upon myself, I need to realise that. This is something that could be avoided if I would just be *normal*. I don't know what's wrong with me.

"No, nothing happened." Summer recoils from my sharp tone, obviously stung by my attitude. I ignore the stab of guilt that shoots through me—I don't have to feel bad. I'm sick of being interrogated.

I'm sick of being me.

"Look, Ingrid, I can't keep doing...*this*"—she gestures between us—"if you're going to keep being like *that*. I want to help you. I want to be there for you, but you need to trust me. You need to let me in."

"I don't want to let anyone in."

"Then don't," Summer answers promptly. "But I can't keep going around in circles anymore. If you don't want to talk about it, then we won't talk about it. Go home and overthink everything and cry about it because I know that's what happens when you hold these things in."

I bite my lip, avoiding her gaze. Summer doesn't dance around the truth; she punches it right in the face. She is brutally honest and doesn't care about the chaos it causes. Usually I appreciate it, but I am one tequila too hung-over to indulge today. And I suppose it's only fair if she doesn't want to indulge in my issues.

"I'm sorry. I'll shut up now."

Summer's face softens a little, but her lips remain pressed together in a tight line. "Look, you need to relax. We're both hot messes right now—I'm pregnant and you're just...*you*." She rolls her eyes and amazingly it makes me feel more at ease. "Right now, we're going to focus on getting your hung-over mind back into action and finding me a dress that is going to fit over my massive stomach."

TODAY, I HIDE in my art. The colours distract me, and I let myself fall into the attention to detail in my thin lines and light shading. I am creating; I am nothing. I let my frustrations escape with lines and shapes and colours and people. I fill pages with beauty and mess and madness. I need to let go. Summer was completely right. I'm killing myself by overthinking this—I don't need this pressure right now. I need to breathe. Last night is coming back in flashes, and with each flashback, my chest gets tighter and tighter. My bedroom walls feel as if they are closing in on me. Leon was making me laugh, touching me *everywhere*, dancing with me...

Between the flashes of Leon, I see Amber. She's rolling her eyes as I stumble towards the bar, giggling as I push a shot towards her, pressing her lips together as she sees Leon grinding against me.

The pressure in my chest tightens, and I throw my pencil down. I can't breathe anymore; I can't think of anything. The memories of Leon are fading, and all I can see is Amber and her ridiculous costume and her mesmerising smile. The way her gaze would capture mine on the dance floor...her huge eyes and full lips. The things that I am trying to avoid, the feelings that are sinking to the very pit of my stomach...

I think about Kat and her undeniable confidence. Her sex appeal and feistiness leaves me breathless. I think about how I felt dancing with her for the first time, letting our bodies come together in the moments of heat.

Those feelings were *deep*.

I can't ignore them anymore. If I shove them down or push them away or let them shy away inside of me, I will explode. I can't hold it anymore. I can't breathe. This pressure on my chest, the tightening in my stomach, the dead weight in my body is killing me. I literally cannot survive like this.

I can't shove it away anymore. I can't hide. I can't run. I can't ignore it. This is it. This is my reality. I don't want to live in this warped reality anymore—I don't want to play make-believe or pretend anymore.

This is who I am.

"SO, THE OTHER night was interesting..." Kat sidles up to me at lunchtime, and I barely have the energy to lift my eyes to meet her curious gaze. I am completely drained. I can't even focus on my schoolwork, let alone my scholarship application. There's too much going on in my mind. Too much to take in.

Of course, I *should* talk about this. Kat of all people should understand. Kat has been through it all, I'm sure. The way she talks about experimenting and how she handles herself...I wish I was like that. I wish I could be like her.

"I guess." I sigh, crushing my apple juice bottle with my fingers. The black nail polish chips off as I tear strips in the label. I feel like this bottle is a representation of me right now. "Where did you and Amber end up?"

My heart hammers as I ask this question. This is the first time I've spoken about Amber since...my realisation, and I feel like Kat can see right through me. It's like she can read my mind and knows of all the craziness going through it.

I shouldn't be embarrassed. I *shouldn't*.

"She came back with me," Kat answers, raising her eyebrows.

My stomach lurches, and I let myself meet her eyes. I don't want to react. Habit and fear and repression tell me to hide my true feelings. Years of shoving it away, tears overflowing in the bathroom, pressing my lips together until they feel numb...it's giving me every tool I need *not* to react. I've had practice at this. I've *got* this. I know this story; I know how it goes.

But I need to admit this. I need to be honest for once in my goddamn life because I owe it to myself. Shoving this down is making me sick. I can't breathe. I can't think. I can't *live* in this hole of secrets. I can't pretend.

"Did you hook up with her?" I ask coolly, fire spreading across my cheeks. I'm banking on Kat's response.

"What if we did? Does it matter to you?" she asks carefully, her full lips turning up in an amused smirk. She's not being rude. In true Kat style, she is observing me, questioning me...testing me.

That is exactly what I need right now. I need this opportunity. I need to be real with her. I need to be real with myself.

"It does actually." My heart hammers in my chest and I can't quite catch my breath, but it doesn't matter because for the first time in *so* long, I am telling the truth. The whole truth. "I like her, Kat."

To my surprise, Kat doesn't react immediately. Her face stays still for a moment as she studies me, her wide eyes taking in my terrified expression. A smile begins to spread across her face. It twitches at the corner of her lips at first, threatening to disappear back behind her resting bitchy expression, but then it spreads, deepening in its authenticity.

"You do? In like an *I want to sleep over and talk about boys* kind of way? Or in like an *I want to sleep over with my body curled up against hers* kind of way?"

Although the fear is threatening to send a panic attack pounding through my nervous body, I can't help but appreciate at her analogy. If there is one thing I love about Kat, it is her way to describe things perfectly.

"The latter," I admit. "Look, you're the first person I've told about this. What happened with Leon was a mistake. I was trying to shove everything away, but I can't pretend anymore." I want to roll my eyes at how cliché I sound, but as soon as I say the words, they feel...*right*. It's true. I can't pretend anymore. It's exhausting; it's overwhelming; it's soul-destroying.

I just want to be me.

Kat's places a gentle hand on my shoulder. "Welcome to the club of being true to yourself. It's a fun club, but the first rule is that we don't make mistakes here. What happened with Leon wasn't a mistake. It opened a door for you—a door to becoming a more authentic version of yourself." She stops for a second as she watches me, waiting for it to sink in. "Of course, I don't know how he's going to feel when he hears that your night with him was what made you come to terms with your lesbian tendencies, but hey, more power to you, sister. Now. What are you gonna do about it?"

I shake my head, unsure of whether to laugh or sob. In a way that only Kat can, she has offended me, empowered me, and terrified me in a matter of five seconds. I don't even know what I'm eating for dinner tonight, let alone what the hell I'm going to do about these unresolved, unexplored feelings for Amber.

"I don't even know whether it's Amber or just...girls." I lower my gaze, trying to ignore the embarrassment. I keep telling myself that I shouldn't be embarrassed. I can't control the desires that are burning deep inside of me; I can't control the way I feel.

"Well, there's only one way to find out." Kat winks, without missing a beat. She doesn't break eye contact, and I wait for the sarcastic grin to spread across her lips. It doesn't.

"Kat, I..."

"Relax. Look, I'm here for you—in whatever capacity you need to be. Drunk make-out buddies, sobbing confused sisters. I'm your friend, Ingrid. I want to look out for you. You trusted me enough to tell me. That's *huge*."

I can tell she's sincere, despite the fact that she's grabbing at the cigarette packet in the back pocket of her ridiculously tight jeans as if it's all she can think about. Kat, if anything, is sincere—always.

"Don't...uh, can you maybe not tell anyone?" I ask hesitantly, not wanting to spoil the moment of unusual tenderness between us. Kat may be tough on her exterior, but to see her being...gentle, it's touching. "I just don't even really know how I feel—"

"Hey, don't worry, I've got you," Kat interrupts. "Your secret is safe with me."

I smile a little, letting the relief flow through me like cool water on a hot summer's day.

Chapter Seven

I ADMIRE THE painting in front of me. The last three weeks have been spent on a cloud of inspiration, relief, and self-exploration. Every time I catch myself repressing my true feelings or criticising the shimmering moments of clarity that flash in front of me, I take a deep breath. This painting is a representation of that breath, the moment I have chosen to love myself. The moment when I don't let fear win anymore, where I accept myself for who I truly am.

With these moments of clarity come moments of confidence. I am yet to talk about my feelings with anyone but Kat—and we haven't even spoken about it since that day in the courtyard—but the past few weeks of accepting my truth and learning to love myself for it have been the kindest gift I could give myself.

Oh, and finally finishing my scholarship portrait.

In the end, the painting didn't have to be of Amber, but it would always represent her and...in a way, it would represent me. This is who I am.

The girl I have painted—the figment of my imagination that has come to life in front of me, is grinning at me through the canvas with a twinkle in her eyes that only I can understand. The slight blush in her cheeks, the teeth that are grazing over her lips with an amused, relaxed expression...it is perfect.

She is perfect.

She is my happiness, my confidence, my acceptance, my truth. She is everything that I hid for too long. She is everything that I love, everything that I want to be, everything that I admire. She is Amber in her beauty. She is Kat in her strength. She is me in her relief.

I couldn't resist the bright pink hair.

I spent so long creating this piece of art that Summer threatened to make a new best friend—although, with her bitchy attitude, constant need for food, spontaneous throwing up, and growing stomach, I don't think I need to worry too much about her following through with *that* particular threat.

I'm finished. I am ready. This is my moment of truth.

On the application, it gives me a space to create a title. I'm guessing they are looking for the *My Dead Grandma* kind of sob stories. I'm not looking to win, or to stand out from the crowd; I just want to be authentic.

So, with shaking fingers and a spinning head, I give my piece of art a title. I name it and I commit. I set it in stone. I am submitting this application; I am taking it further. I am taking *myself* further. I want to be better, do better, live better.

Everything else is complete. I filled out this application the first day I finally got the courage to print it. I didn't want to back out. I didn't want to give up. I was so scared. I was terrified.

My eyes trail down to the title, and I'm smiling so hard that it hurts. My piece of art sits in front of me, polished and ready. This is it. One more glance, before I fold my application carefully and slide it into its envelope. My artwork gleams at me, as if shining with the passion that made it come to life. She is beautiful. She is pink-haired, blue-eyed, red-lipped, and covered in overalls. She has black nail polish and no shoes and a casual stance, as if she doesn't have a care in the world.

She is *Truth*.

I'M NOT SCARED to tell Summer. In fact, my only fear is that the excitement of confirming her suspicions may put her into preterm labour. We sit at our usual café, while she scarfs down her usual double order of pancakes and eggs. She's getting big now, and we're meant to go dress shopping after our breakfast, so I may as well fill her with some kind of happiness before we get in front of those unforgivable store mirrors.

"So, I have something to tell you," I begin, before taking a calming sip of my overly strong coffee.

She glances up at me sharply, eyes narrowed. Of course, she knows something is up. Summer always knows. But despite her nagging, constant text messages, and 'surprising' me at my house while I worked on my RMIT application, she still couldn't get to the bottom of it.

"You got into RMIT?" she gasps.

"It's way too early to hear back from them, I only just submitted! You'll be the first to know about that, though," I reassure her.

She frowns, studying me carefully. Her cheeks have become fuller lately, and I always rolled my eyes when I heard the term "pregnancy glow," but I can see it on her now. She is radiant.

"You're not pregnant, are you? Because I don't think I can share the spotlight right now."

I roll my eyes. For once, Summer is *completely* off the mark, and finally, I'm all too happy to correct her.

"I'm not pregnant, Summer. I'm a lesbian."

Her mouth drops, and her fork clatters onto the plate with a loud clang that causes our neighbours at the next table to shoot furtive glances at us. I start laughing, and suddenly, Summer is wheezing for breath as she giggles with me. She clutches her stomach, and tears stream down her cheeks as she explodes in hysterics. We're lost in the moment together—it's relief and pure joy.

The people look at us in earnest now, with perturbed looks on their snotty faces and unimpressed glances at their partners. I don't care, let them stare, let them see how happy we are. A pregnant teenager and a delinquent lesbian with pink hair—we don't care, let them frown.

Finally, Summer calms down just enough that through gasps for air and fits of laughter, she asks me, "Are you lying?"

For the first time in so long, I'm not lying. I don't need to lie anymore. I don't need to have that weight on my chest and that fear creeping over my shoulder.

"I'm not," I answer. "I promise."

She takes a few deep breaths, as the chuckles cascade through her body before slowly subsiding. "I'm so glad you finally came to terms with it. Look, I always knew, Ingrid. But it wasn't my place to push. Even though, I guess I did kind of push you...sometimes."

"I know. Thank you."

This time, she rolls her eyes. "Don't be ridiculous, you don't have to thank me for anything. Actually, yeah, maybe you can thank me for all the times I bit my tongue when I so desperately wanted to call you out for leering at Amber."

I chuckle dryly, although the comment hits a little too close to home and my seriousness overcomes me. "Look, Amber doesn't know yet.

Actually, you and Kat are the only ones who know—Kat kind of figured it out on her own. I don't want this to be like a *big thing*, and I definitely don't want Amber to feel uncomfortable since she doesn't even like girls. So maybe just let me figure out where I go next before you start openly joking about it?"

Summer suddenly turns deadly serious, and a flash of sadness glints in her blue eyes. "I'd never do anything to make you—or anyone—feel uncomfortable, Ingrid! I hated seeing you sad, like you weren't being the real you. I'm with you one hundred percent, and my lips are sealed. It's your choice who you want to tell and how you want to tell them, but for the record, I don't think Amber just likes boys, if you know what I mean."

"It doesn't matter. I'm just coming to terms with everything, and I need to spend time on myself before I bring anyone else into the picture. That starts with telling everyone—which I will. Just, on my terms."

"Can you tell Jackson soon? He's becoming broody, and this would definitely cheer him up."

"Of course, I can, but I don't want my coming out to be some kind of anecdotal story to cheer people up. Why is he broody?"

"I don't know." Summer admits. "I guess it's just the whole baby thing and trying to figure out what he's doing with his life."

"Give him time, this is a lot for him. We talked about him staying with me if things got tense at yours."

"About that..." Summer begins, looking up at me from underneath her full eyelashes. I know that look. It's the look she gives me before she asks me to do her a favour—the look that she *thinks* no one can resist.

"Yes?"

"Can he come and stay with you for a while, Ingrid? He's driving me insane. I'm too pregnant for his shit right now." She pouts and cradles her stomach.

"Of course, he can. I offered in the first place."

She lights up and begins scarfing down the rest of her pancakes. "Thank you, Ingrid," she says through a mouth full of syrup. "You're amazing. I told him that he can meet us after we go dress shopping to talk to you about it."

Summer is talkative through the rest of breakfast until we make our way to the dress shop. Finding a dress for her mother's wedding isn't something that she's been looking forward to—especially because of her growing belly but also because of how she feels about her new stepdad.

My job is to keep her mood upbeat enough for us to find a dress that works for her. I need her to feel comfortable on the day.

The minute we walk into the dress shop and head to the maternity racks, Summer's frown deepens. I can see the negative thoughts coming in stormy crashes behind her eyes. With every dress that she rejects, she becomes moodier and moodier.

"Look, Summer, I'm trying to help you, but you are going to have at least try *something* on," I say, trying to remain calm as Summer pouts and turns away from the dress rack for the fifth time. She gazes wistfully at the "normal" sizes, and I don't bother telling her that I—the nonpregnant friend—would probably need to be wearing a maternity dress just to fit in these clothes.

"I'm going to look ridiculous and feel like shit anyway," she mumbles. "What's the point? This is a waste of time."

I watch her until she finally meets my eyes. I don't want to stand here arguing all day, but I also don't want the inevitable breakdown that will come if we put off finding this dress any longer. We've already had two cancelled shopping trips. I cannot fail her today. We need to find her a damn dress.

"Fine," I say. "Let's just go to another shop—maybe one that you don't have to take out a fucking mortgage just to afford one of their dresses."

Summer laughs nervously and ushers me out of the shop. I'll do anything to take her attention away from those negative thoughts. We walk into a more budget-friendly and well-known store, and Summer immediately finds more options here.

"I think I'll feel better if you try something on too," she says. "You're gonna need a dress anyway."

She is still convinced that I'm going to be a better date than Jackson, and I don't bother arguing because I know better than to argue with the pregnant girl.

"Fine," I say.

We sift through the dresses for a while. I'm pleased to see Summer holding a few options draped over her arm as we head to the change room.

Summer's dresses range from potato sack to definitely not zipping up. Finally, she finds a peach-coloured, mid-length dress. It's slim fitting but stretchy material—so it will definitely still fit her as her bump grows bigger before her mum's wedding. It hugs her hips and little bump perfectly, and I even catch her taking a photo of herself in the mirrors.

"Hey, I look cute." She turns to the side and cradling her stomach.

I lean back against the change-room door as my best friend finally embraces her changing body. She admires herself, tossing her hair back, pushing out her boobs—which are huge now.

She twirls in front of the mirror to see the backside view, smiling even more. I laugh as she poses and contorts her body, seemingly amazed that she can be hot *and* pregnant.

"I can't believe I'm pregnant," she says, suddenly soft. She looks at herself and then at her stomach, touching it gently, as if it will break open. "Ingrid, there's a *baby* inside of me."

I snort. "I'm glad you're figuring that out now; otherwise, you'll have a nasty shock in about five months."

"No, seriously." She gasps, turning to face me. "I'm having a baby!"

"Yes, you are!"

"We find out if it's a boy or a girl next week. I can't believe it. It's happening so quickly."

I walk over and wrap my arm around her shoulder, staring at the pair of us in the mirror. She can't seem to take her hands off her stomach and is staring at it in awe.

"I guess you could say things are going pretty well for us then?" I ask.

My pink hair is ridiculously messy today, teamed with no makeup and this over-the-top formal dress, and I look hilarious. But mostly, I look happy.

Summer does too.

"I guess they are."

JACKSON AND I lay sprawled on opposite sides of the couch, our feet clashing for that cherished middle space. He shoves chips into his mouth as if he hasn't eaten for weeks and laughs mindlessly at whatever ridiculous trash is playing on the TV.

I've been scrolling through the old pictures on my phone for an hour now, staring at myself, studying myself. I'm trying to see what's changed, why I look so different now. Of course, the pink hair is the most obvious change, but for some reason, I've become more confident over the past year. The way I dress, the way I stand, how I pose for photos... it's all different.

"You haven't really said much about the whole lesbian thing," I say, glancing up at Jackson.

"There's not much to say," he responds. "I was actually more surprised you let me take you up on your offer of staying here for a while. I think we all saw it coming. Or should I say, coming *out*?" He snorts and so do I.

"Except me." I chuckle.

"Apparently not." He grins. "I think it's great. You seem happier now already."

"I am," I answer. "I really am."

He flicks off the TV and turns his full attention to me. His eyes are dull—devoid of his usual spark and excitement.

"I'm getting really stressed out, Ingrid."

I sigh and let my foot rest against his, trying to be comforting. "I can see that. Summer said things are getting kind of tense for you guys right now. Look, I know this is stressful, but I also have no idea what it's like to suddenly become a parent at seventeen, so you need to tell me what I can do to help you. Both of you guys have helped me *so* much through all of this. I want to help you guys as much as I can."

Jackson runs a hand through his wild hair. "I don't know what you can do to help. I don't even know what *I* can do to help. I have no idea what I'm doing."

"Neither do I," I admit. "My biggest decisions right now revolve around food or what I want to draw and that's about as intense as it gets. I don't blame you for feeling lost."

"But I want to be there for her! I want to be a good dad—I want to do this right. How can I do that when neither of us have a stable life, or income? We're *not* parents. It's like we're two teenagers playing make-believe. I'm sick of pretending. I want to be real. I want to be there for her, but I can't do that when I can't even afford a freaking car seat for my baby. And she's not *letting* me. She's blocking me out, Ingrid. I'm not even invited to the wedding."

"I think this wedding is going to be a lot harder for her than she wants to admit. She's been through a lot with her mum, and right now, that tension is at an all-time high. She's only just coming to terms with this pregnancy and the fact that you guys are actually going to have a *baby*. Give it time," I tell Jackson reassuringly, trying to make him feel at ease. His expression remains stony. "Look, the only thing you can do right now is focus on what *you* need to be doing. Are you applying for a scholarship at RMIT?"

Jackson turns from stony to offended. He juts out his chin and rolls his eyes. "Are you kidding? Me trying to go up against people like you? No way. Besides, I need a job right now—not an education. That can come later, if I want."

"Then what do you want to do?" I ask. "What's your dream job? Think big. Don't worry about logistics—we'll figure that out later."

A smile flickers on Jackson's lips, and his eyes glaze over as he looks into a future that I can't seem to comprehend right now. "I want to *draw*, Ingrid," he tells me wistfully. "I want to create comics; I want to make people laugh... I want to make *kids* laugh. I want to create the things that I wished I could see and experience as I was growing up."

"Like what?" I ask, enjoying this moment of artistic passion glinting in my dark living room. For the first time ever, Jackson is being optimistic about his future career goals—I can see him having a choice.

"Like movies." He murmurs. "And characters. Comic books and little TV shows. About anything and everything. About adventure and optimism and growing up and...love."

"Then do it. Create it. Create what you're dreaming about, and the rest will fall into place. Even if it means getting a shitty job and drawing comics in between serving customers. You *can* do both, until one day, you have it all. One day, you will be doing what you love. I promise."

Jackson beams by the end of my little speech. "You know, for someone who has so many problems, you sure are good at fixing other people's problems."

"Hey, I'm fixing my problems, thank you very much. Everything is kind of working out for the best."

"I guess it is," Jackson whispers, as if he's scared to be too hopeful.

I know the feeling.

I DOWN THE shot of tequila, trying not to laugh as Kat sways beside me. What better way to celebrate another week of surviving at school and opening myself up to a new world of possibilities than at Cloud Nine? It's just us tonight—although, I didn't miss her swiping away a text from Leon. She's looking out for me, and I appreciate that. Right now, being near Leon again in my fragile state is probably not the best idea. He is a lovely guy and I did have fun with him, but I'm figuring myself out right now.

Jackson is spending the night with Summer, and I didn't want to sit at home alone. I want to be free; I want to explore; I want to have fun.

And right now, I am very much satisfied with standing with Kat in the middle of this club filled with beautiful women. Right now, I'm not holding back. I'm becoming a truer version of myself. I'm letting myself explore these feelings. With no pressure, no judgement, no fear. This is me, and this is what I want.

Kat drags me back to the dance floor and twirls me around, giggling as I let my hands slip between her fingers. She isn't as drunk as I am and she shoots curious glances at me as our bodies get closer and the beat gets louder.

I don't think I want to hook up with Kat tonight. Then again, I've spent so long shutting my thoughts down and ignoring my feelings that I don't know what I want anymore. I'm not so drunk that I can't make my decisions. But my curiosity and sudden freedom drives me closer to her, makes me grip her hips just that little bit tighter—a little bit too tight to just be fun and flirty now. She looks good tonight, in a casual black dress and army combat boots. Her hair is piled into a messy bun on the top of her head, with bright blue twirling in with mahogany brown.

The sweat drips down the back of my neck as the music takes control of my body. I fall into the thumping of the bass, screaming the lyrics into Kat's face, letting my body bounce with the beat. She giggles, gripping my waist and thrusting her body against the beat of the music. Her body convulses and moves impossibly fast as she tries to keep up when the bass drops. She leads me in our dance moves, alternating from crazy spasms to seductive grinding. No dance move is too corny or too controversial for us.

The dancing funnels out my frustrations. I smash my body against the beat and it smashes me back. All of the agony of hiding myself away, shoving my true feelings down pours out with my sweat. I become one with the music. I become one with myself.

At some point, I begin grinding against Kat in earnest. My hands wander against her body, and I shut off the ever-shrinking part of my brain that tells me this is wrong. For the first time in my life, I do what feels right. I let myself appreciate the beauty of the female body—of *Kat's* body.

The skin exposed on her bare shoulders is soft. Her waist is small and flexible as she moves in my grip, shaking her head with the music. I drop my head onto her neck, inhaling her scent, appreciating the way it fits perfectly. *We* fit perfectly.

"Do you want to kiss me?" she breathes and turns slowly in my arms until her face is touching mine. Our sweaty foreheads connect, and her breath brushes my cheeks.

"Yes," I gasp, pushing my body further into her. I pull her closer, and my anxieties fall away, allowing me to feel the moment.

We remain still for a moment as the club continues to explode around us. The beat thunders against me and the dance floor is filled, but in that moment, we lock eyes. Kat beams down at me and I take it in, every inch of her face. I let myself fall. I allow myself to take the plunge.

I let myself be free.

Kat doesn't move. Her eyes flicker nervously as she watches me. I don't concentrate on the fact that I make Kat nervous—something I never imagined was possible—or the fact that the drumbeat thunders through my body in a way that makes me want to drag Kat out of this club and take her straight back to my house.

Without another glance, I close the gap between us. I plunge into the unknown as my lips connect with her soft ones. She responds immediately, pulling me closer, reassuringly wrapping her arms around my neck as we continue to sway with the music, never escaping too far from the beat.

Her lips are like fire, and as my tongue slips between them, the fire explodes in my body. The cold metal of her tongue piercing sends chills cascading through my body, and my tongue glides over it. I push my body against hers, and my hands slip below her waist as the kiss deepens.

This is *right*. This is everything.

SUDDENLY, THE ROOM is spinning, and I can't quite catch my breath because Kat pushes me up against her bedroom door, lining my neck with gentle kisses. She has tucked her hands under my dress, resting just above my waist, grazing her fingers against my skin.

I fall into her embrace, noticing the chills that dance up my spine as she brushes her fingers against me, noticing that my heart feels as if it's about to pound out of my chest and my breath comes out in short gasps.

"Do you...do you want to go further?" She pulls away, watching me carefully. She is breathing hard too. I can feel the urgency in her grip as she presses her body against mine.

"I... This is okay, for now," I breathe. "Is that okay?"

She nods, pressing her forehead against mine and letting out a soft chuckle that breezes straight into my lips. "Of course, it's okay. Anything is okay." With what seems like a great effort, she untangles herself from my grip, loosely grabs my hand, and pulls me into her bedroom. Even just her fingers brushing against the inside of my wrist sends tingles dancing up my arm. "Do you want something to wear? Some pyjamas? I don't want you to feel uncomfortable."

Her voice is so gentle, so *careful*. It's a completely new side of the dominant, aggressive Kat that I've become accustomed to. I raise my eyebrows in amusement as she searches through her dresser, whilst keeping her other hand firmly entwined in mine.

"Yeah. Just a baggy shirt will be fine. I guess I'm sleeping over."

She turns around sharply, looking alarmed. "Do you want to go home? I can call a taxi for you."

I don't miss the flicker of disappointment as I take my hand away from hers and collapse onto her surprisingly comfortable bed. "Kat. You need to relax. You're freaking out more than me."

Suddenly, her shoulders slump with relief, and she throws a grey shirt at me, laughing loudly. "I'm just trying to make you comfortable. I don't want you to rush into anything or make any mistakes."

"I thought the first rule of our little club was that there are no mistakes." I wink. In a bold movement, I pull my tight dress over my head. I am completely exposed—sitting in my underwear on Kat's bed. I enjoy the shock that overshadows her face. I take my time unravelling her shirt—seriously, how big is this shirt?—and she watches me. My plain white bra and panties are nothing special, but it doesn't matter because for a moment, I am putting it all out there.

Finally, I tug the shirt over my head. Kat giggles nervously and I pull her onto the bed. She can't take her eyes off me, and I become nervous under her intense expression.

"Kat, I am perfectly comfortable. You're not taking advantage of me, if that's what you're worried about. You need to stop worrying and start acting like yourself because that's freaking me out more than anything."

Kat laughs a little, placing her hands on my bare thighs and stroking at the skin nervously. "I guess..."

"Well, what would the *real* Kat do in this situation?" I push, raising my eyebrows at her. "Right now, I just want this to be an authentic experience, so I want you to act how you usually do."

She jerks back, looking shocked. I'm sure that I've given this girl heart palpitations multiple times tonight. "Ingrid, are you sure? Don't you want to just go at your pace? This is all new—"

"Stop!" I giggle, pushing a finger to her lips to shut her up. "I want you to be yourself. I want *you*. So, if the next words that come out of your mouth aren't completely and authentically *Kat*, then I'll be taking this ridiculously big shirt and leaving you here in bed."

For a moment, we are still; silently challenging each other as Kat seems to consider her options. Finally, without breaking eye contact, in one swift movement, she wraps her lips around my finger and sucks hard. I can't help the moan that escapes my lips.

She breaks into a smile, releases my finger, and stands up to pull her dress over her head quickly, revealing a tiny red bra and a matching G-string. "You want me to be myself? Here it is."

Without hesitating, she throws her body down on top of me, pushing me back onto the bed. She straddles my hips with her bare legs and kisses me before I can fully comprehend what is happening. She slips her tongue in my mouth and presses her body against mine. I fall into this moment. *This* is what I wanted—for her to show me how she felt. I didn't want her to be scared or to tiptoe around my feelings. I spent long enough tiptoeing around my own feelings, avoiding them and awkwardly shoving them away.

I want to kiss this girl, so I'm going to kiss this girl.

I WAKE UP curled in Kat's arms. Her hair is matted around my face, and I've been drooling on her shoulder. I've loosely wrapped my arms around her waist, and for a moment, I take in the warmth between us. I relish in the comfort of lying quietly next to her. It just feels *right*.

She breathes softly, and I shuffle away from her a little so I can properly look at her face. She's just as vulnerable as she was last night. With every breath, her hair flutters away from her mouth before falling back onto her lips.

I swear, only Kat can make sleeping in last night's makeup look stunning.

She begins to stir, and I curl back into her arms. This only seems to wake her up more, and suddenly, she mumbles a husky "good morning" into my neck.

"Morning."

Immediately, she pulls away from me, eyes wide. "You're still here," she gasps.

I'm amused as she sleepily tries to take in the situation. No doubt, there are memories of last night passing through her mind. "No one has ever stayed before."

"I guess I'm different."

"I guess you are." She giggles.

"So...last night..." I start. I can't help it. I'm a chronic overthinker. Summer constantly jokes that she needs to sew my lips shut, but I'm starting to think she really should.

"Last night was..." Kat chews her lip thoughtfully. "Whatever you want it to be."

"What do you mean?" With the harsh daylight comes the rays of self-doubt and confusion. Does this mean I like Kat? Or did I just want to share my first girl-kiss with her?

It never went any further than kissing, but could it in the future? Do I want it to go further? I want to shove my head under the pillow and hide away from these confronting thoughts. It is too early, and I am too hung-over.

"I mean...if you just wanted to get it out of your system, that's cool. No hard feelings if you never want to be like that with me again. If you just want to chill with me and see where it goes, that's cool too. I don't want to push you."

"I seem to remember forcing you out of that mindset last night," I say, pushing the limits. I notice a slight blush creep across Kat's cheeks, but she seems to control it. "You really are a cool girl, you know?"

She rolls her eyes. "Come on. After that kiss last night, you could at least call me *hot*."

I burst into laughter, and Kat follows suit. What is it that they say? Oh yeah, laughter is the best medicine. Surely, that must apply to hangovers too.

Chapter Eight

SUMMER GRIPS HER stomach so tightly that I'm afraid she might do some damage to the baby. I never liked coming to doctor's offices, but I sit next to her with Jackson on the other side, feeling privileged enough to be invited to this important appointment. In less than twenty minutes, Summer will know if she is having a boy or a girl.

I fidget nervously, chipping off my black nail polish and wringing my fingers in between each other. I can't stop thinking about last night. Which makes me think of Amber, which makes my stomach drop.

"Jesus, anyone would think you're having the baby," Summer mutters in annoyance. I don't recoil from her harsh tone because I don't blame her for being nervous. "God, I wish I could drink tequila right now."

I snort, ignoring the way the other patients whip their heads over to stare at us. "I don't know if you're little one would appreciate it." I grin. "And who wants to drink tequila at ten in the morning?"

"I would, though."

Slowly, Summer begins to crack a grin, looking down at her stomach. She pushes her "normal" clothes to the limits now. Her normally baggy white T-shirt is straining against her bump, threatening to tear at the seams. "So, final guesses. What do we think I'm having?"

"Boy!" Jackson answers immediately. The enthusiasm is clear in his voice, and I can't help but smile at his excitement.

"I think it's a boy too."

"I guess I'm the only one for Team Girl." I sigh. "Of course, we shouldn't be surprised by that."

Summer and Jackson roll their eyes. The truth is, I know Summer doesn't really care about the gender of her baby—as long as it's healthy. I know that she is young and this is scary, but I also know that she is going to be a great mum and Jackson is going to be a great dad. I'm just lucky enough to come along for the ride.

"Summer Stevens?"

We all jump up and make our way for the ultrasound room. Summer chews at her lip and anxiously clutches her stomach, and I know it's mostly excitement that is fuelling her nerves.

"If you could pop up onto the bed and unbutton your pants, the technician will be with you shortly."

Summer jumps onto the bed faster than I've seen her move for a while now, and Jackson and I drag chairs on either side of the bed. She grips both of our hands nervously, staring at the screen where the ultrasound will be performed.

"I can't wait," she gasps, breathless with excitement. "We're going to see our baby."

She smiles up at Jackson, and he beams down at her. I press my lips shut and let them share this moment of terror and excitement and *life*.

"Okay!" An older-looking man bursts into the room, clapping his hands together. His hair is a shock of white that stands out even in this dark room. "My name is Michael. It looks like we're going to find out the gender of your baby today, Summer. Hopefully, the little one is cooperating!"

She beams at him, immediately pulling her shirt up over her stomach. I can tell she is more than eager for this. "Yes please."

"Well..." He shifts down onto a chair and pulls the monitor towards him. "Let's get this started then. Now, the gel is going to feel a little cold, but you should be used to that by now." He smiles, putting her at ease immediately. "This is your first baby?"

"Yeah, it is," Summer replies, shifting as he squirts the blue gel onto her stomach and moves the wand around. Her attention is glued to the screen, and her expression lights up as soon as she catches sight of her baby.

I'm in awe as he points out the heartbeat and the face. It really does look like a baby now—not just a little dot anymore. Summer's eyes glint in the dark, and she seems to be getting closer and closer to tears as he points out every perfect little thing about her baby: ten fingers, ten toes, perfect little legs and arms...

"Well, it's a girl," he says suddenly, turning to point at the screen. "See those three lines? That's definitely a vagina."

Summer bursts into tears, and Jackson lets out a little sniffle. My cheeks hurt from smiling as they fall in love with their daughter. I secretly thought the pictures all looked the same—kind of like an alien—but I can make out Summer's baby now. She's so cute.

Summer grips my hand tightly as Jackson leans down to kiss her. Their tears mingle with each other, and I just sit there, feeling like nothing could possibly be wrong with the world when happiness like this exists.

"I GUESS YOU submitted your application to RMIT then?"

My heart almost explodes out of my chest when I whirl around to see Amber leaning casually against the door frame. Of course, I'm the only one here—what kind of art students actually come to an optional class on a Monday morning? Even Jackson is nowhere to be seen.

"I sure have," I answer, not trusting myself to expand any further. I need to get it together. I can't act like a nervous wreck every time I see her, and there is no tequila in sight so I'm just going to have to tough this one out.

"So, what are you working on now?" Amber waltzes over to me and settles just behind me, leaning over my shoulder to inspect my canvas. With her closeness comes the waft of her overly sweet perfume, and I can hardly catch my breath.

"It's something just for fun. I want to get into watercolours, and I thought what better way than with bright flowers? I want to give it to Summer and Jackson if it turns out good enough," I say, forcing my voice to remain calm.

"For the baby?"

"Yeah," I say. Summer's pregnancy is public knowledge now—it's not like she could hide it any longer. "Do you like it?"

I turn around and attempt to casually lean against the desks behind me. As always, there's a shadow of amusement dancing on her full lips.

"Of course. I like all of your art, Ingrid." Her eyes twinkle as she watches the inevitable blush creep across my cheeks. Does she know how nervous she makes me? *Does she like it?* "So, are you looking forward to the wedding?"

I raise my eyebrows in confusion. Had I mentioned that to her and completely forgotten? Or am I just literally going insane now? "I guess... How did you know about that? I knew that you and Jackson were friends, but you and Summer aren't exactly best buddies."

"I'm Mark's niece," she tells me. "Of course, Summer wouldn't know that because they don't really get along. So, I'm going to be at the wedding too. I'll be singing at the reception, actually."

A genuine smile spreads across my face. I'm not going to hold back anymore. I'm sick of holding back. I've worked so hard to get to this point. Why *shouldn't* I be allowed to show her my genuine reaction?

"To be honest, that makes me a little more excited about going," I say, with barely a quiver in my voice. "I'll have a drinking buddy after you're done performing."

Amber laughs, and her mahogany hair falls across her face. Her curls are wild today—completely untouched by any hairspray or even a hairbrush. I can imagine her jumping out of the shower and letting them dry naturally. I wrench my eyes shut, shoving the image of her in the shower out of my mind—it's not the time.

"I wanted to talk about that, actually..." She lowers her eyes to her entwined hands, looking suddenly nervous. I raise my eyebrows, shocked to see any kind of insecurity falling over the girl that can't be cracked.

"Yes?" I ask, equally nervous. God, why am *I* nervous now?

"I had so much fun with you the other night. Actually, I go to Cloud Nine quite frequently—you know, choirboys and all. I saw you there with Kat last week." All of the air leaves my body in one big huff, and I shove my shaking hands in the pockets of my jeans. This isn't where I saw this conversation going. "You guys...I guess you're a thing now? I didn't even know you liked girls..."

"It's a new revelation," I say coolly, feeling suddenly confident. I don't think she's jealous, but it doesn't matter. I want to talk about it. "We were just drunk and having fun. We're not a thing."

"You're not dating?" She looks up, chewing her lip as she asks this question.

I shake my head, forming the sentences in my mind before they tumble out of my mouth. "Nope. I'm single." I hesitate, tasting my next sentence on my lips, rolling it over my tongue as I consider it. "But I do like girls, yeah."

"Oh, okay."

"Yeah."

The silence settles between us, and I take my time to build up my confidence again. I was thrown off guard by Amber's questioning but keep my breaths even as I force my thundering heart to calm down.

"Look, I was planning on forcing Jackson to come out with me this Friday. I really want to cheer him up and maybe convince him to crash this wedding to keep Summer happy. Did you want to join?" I don't know where my sudden boldness comes from, or even how I managed to make up this story in less than ten seconds, but I am immediately impressed with myself. This is far better than being a blithering idiot.

"Will Kat be there?" Amber asks.

I keep my face very still, so that she doesn't notice the fall in my expression. Maybe she's interested in Kat. And that has to be okay. I press my lips together, falling deeper into the plans that I invented ten seconds ago.

"Maybe. I haven't asked her. Did you want to ask her?"

"I was just wondering," Amber answers.

"I'll ask her. She always knows how to have a good time."

"I could see that."

"What about Leon? Did you like him?" I ask. Again, I'm impressed by how casual I manage to manipulate my voice into sounding.

"I think you liked him a little more than I did." Amber winks, and I laugh nervously. "No, he was a good time. We should definitely invite him too—make a night out of it. On one condition."

"What?" I ask, frantically trying to see where I went wrong in my little made-up ploy to get Amber to come out with me. Did she see right through it?

"You have to do more shots with me. That was *fun.*"

"I think I can manage that. Hey, do you have any gigs this week? I'd love to watch you sing."

"Oh, coming out in the open now?" I don't miss the innuendo dripping from her lips. "Not going to hide in the back of the room anymore, sneakily watching me sing? You know, I can kind of tell that you watch my videos too. There's always one viewer from our town who seems to watch them as soon as I post them—and since you're always online on Facebook that time, I kind of put two and two together..."

Instead of letting the brewing ball of anxiety in my stomach explode, I take a deep, slow breath. I've learnt a lot about truth over this past month, and I am more than ready to be truthful in all aspects of my life now—even if it scares the hell out of me.

"Yeah, you caught me." I sigh. "Look, I think we established that I was kind of jealous of you. You're just doing so well for yourself, you're so...

confident. I guess it kind of inspired me to pick up my game with my art. You're a great singer, too."

"Well, I'm glad that you've turned that jealousy around. And to answer your question, I do have a gig. Tomorrow, actually. It's not going to be anything huge—just a little entertainment for a function at one of the venues on the wharf. It's an open house, so you're welcome to come along." She pauses, studying me carefully. "But no standing at the back, okay? I want you to make your presence known."

"I think I can manage that. I'll be the one squealing for you, front and centre. I might bring Summer along; I think she'll like that. She feels like she's missing out on a lot lately. Maybe you guys can kind of get to know each other?"

"I would like that." Amber beams. "I'd like it a lot."

"THIS IS A date," Summer sings. "This is *so* a date."

"Yeah, for you and Jackson maybe." I roll my eyes as Jackson laughs, wrapping his arms around Summer's bare shoulders. Even though the night air is cool, Summer is dressed in a tight white dress that clings to her every curve. She was more than a little excited to be getting out of the house, now that the morning sickness has subsided. I'm sure Amber will be more than impressed with our little crowd.

"I can't believe you actually *asked* her if you could come," Jackson says. "Jesus, Ingrid, you're like a completely different person."

"I'm not different," I tell him. "I'm just letting myself do what I want for the first time in my life, and right now, that involves watching Amber sing. Out in the open. I'm sick of hiding in the dark."

"I'm...coming out," Summer sings. "I-I'm coming out."

I burst into laughter at her ridiculous singing, but truthfully, the presence of Summer and Jackson eases my nerves. I'm ashamed to admit how long I spent in front of the mirror, painstakingly applying just the right shade of maroon lipstick and trying to find a dress that best accentuated my butt—it's my best feature, of course. In the end, I settled for a tight black peplum dress that flows over the hips but is tight around the butt. My pink hair is untamed and wild around my shoulders. The colour pops vibrantly against the black dress.

I catch Jackson staring at Summer, and I don't blame him. She looks stunning. I know that this pregnancy and her changing body has been tough on her, but embracing the reality of their baby girl has been the most beautiful thing in the world.

We enter the venue right on time. Amber's set is supposed to start at seven o'clock exactly. She's talking in the microphone already, warming up the large crowd. We round the corner into the stage area, and I stop dead, desperately trying to compose myself.

"*Jesus*," I mutter.

"Keep your bloody pants on," Summer hisses, dragging me to an empty table near the front of the room. Amber meets my gaze almost immediately, breaking into a huge smile.

I can't take my eyes off her. She looks... *Ugh*. I chew into my bottom lip as I take in her outfit, desperately trying not to look like a creep. Her dress is actually quite similar to mine, but the deep red in it brings out the auburn in her hair. Her curls cascade around her shoulders and around her face. She looks beautiful.

"You sure know how to pick 'em." Jackson grins next to me.

Amber is still talking, but I'm not, for the life of me, taking in what she is saying because I can't stop staring at her lips. She must know. She must be able to see me leering. I need to relax and stop being so crazy.

"Let me get you a drink," Summer says, one step ahead of me. "I'm getting water, but do you want something alcoholic?"

I shake my head. "Just a lemonade, please." I'm not that thirsty; I just need something to do with my hands.

As Summer strides over to the bar, Amber starts singing and the rest of the room falls away. I don't even know if Jackson is sitting next to me. Summer could literally go into labour right now, and I wouldn't know about it because I'm at the front of this room, while Amber lilts a slow, hopeful song filled with love and optimism. Her voice echoes off the glass walls of the venue, falling into rhythm with the crashing waves outside. As she sings, her body sways with the music, and I watch her, awed.

"Ingrid." Jackson shoves his elbow into me. "You need to stop drooling."

I laugh nervously before turning my full attention on Amber and pressing my lips firmly shut. Summer arrives back to the table with the drinks, and I take mine immediately, letting the cool glass calm my nerves.

She has the attention of the entire room in the palm of her hand as she sings. She controls our emotions, our mood, everything. She commands her power as she belts out the lyrics, lifting her hands in the air, putting every ounce of strength into this song. A smile slowly spreads across my face as she sings. I take in every movement, every expression, every lilt in her flawless voice.

After the first song, the room explodes into applause. Beside me, Jackson whistles loudly, and I let out an excited squeal, clapping my hands together. I want her to see that I'm impressed. I want her to get the reaction she deserves.

She beams as she launches into her next song, capturing our attention straight away. Even Summer and Jackson sit silently as she performs, watching her create stories with the lyrics and send emotion and passion vibrating through the audience.

Beside me, Summer jerks suddenly. Her eyes widen and her hands fly to her stomach, staring down. She looks terrified.

"What's wrong?" I ask. "What happened?"

Amber continues singing, capturing the attention of the room as she belts out the lyrics. Summer remains frozen, unable to answer the question; her eyes are as wide as saucers.

"Oh my god," she gasps. "She's kicking, guys! She's kicking."

Both Jackson and I place our hands on Summer's swollen stomach. Jackson looks almost as scared as Summer does. Although, I can't seem to feel anything other than a small stirring under my hand, Summer is beaming down at her stomach as if it's the most incredible thing in the world. Amber's voice surrounds us as Summer and Jackson grasp her belly, smiling through the tears.

I turn back to Amber, deciding to let them enjoy their moment of joy and life and creation. Amber meets my gaze as her song reaches its climax. By the look on her face, I can tell that she knows what's happening. She is watching us as she sings, letting the lyrics fall over us and the magic of her music become a soundtrack to this beautiful moment.

For the rest of the set, Summer and Jackson remain grasping her stomach, and my attention remains locked on Amber. She creates worlds of beauty and sadness and exploration and strength with her lyrics. I choke up when her ballads reach the point of no return and her lyrics become a melody of sadness and change. Summer is beaming at Amber, seemingly forgetting any tension that was ever between them as her fingers trail along her stomach.

The chills cascade over me as I embrace this rare moment of clarity, enjoying the unexpected chaos of life and the sweet taste of resolve. Summer feeling her baby kick for the first time as I fall into this crazy tunnel of admiration for the girl that sings in front of us... This is perfect.

After the set, Amber strides over to us, smiling from ear to ear. Although the songs seemed to be musically demanding, and Amber belted them out seemingly with every ounce of strength she had, she seems to be invigorated. Her skin is almost as radiant as her smile.

"I saw you guys as I was singing," she says, by way of greeting. "What happened? Did you feel your baby kick?"

"Yeah. For the first time," Summer answers, still clutching her stomach. "Actually, she was kicking all the way through your performance. You have some killer vocals. She must've loved it as much as we did."

"Oh, it's a girl? Congratulations! As soon as I heard you were pregnant, I was hoping for a girl. There aren't enough girls in the family," Amber rambles, taking a seat beside me.

I brace myself for the tension that comes with Amber's side of the family, but Summer doesn't seem fazed at all. In fact, she seems more caught up in raising her eyebrows subtly at me as Amber mentions her hope for a girl. I guess I wasn't the only one on Team Girl after all.

"You were amazing up there," I finally manage to choke out. "Seriously, Amber. I think that's the best performance I've seen you give."

"I had a pretty awesome muse," she says, meeting my gaze.

Jackson clears his throat, and I turn sharply towards him. "Look, it's getting late. I should get this mama home. I'm sure she's just going to want to talk to her stomach for the rest of the night anyway."

"Something like that. I heard you guys are all heading out to the club on Friday night? Jackson can stay with me afterwards if you want to crash at Ingrid's house, Amber."

I bite down hard on my lip, suppressing any reaction at Summer's matchmaking skills. I have to give her props for her suggestion, though, and my nervous giggle slips out before I can gain control of it.

"Oh, I didn't realise Jackson was staying with you, Ingrid," Amber says. "Don't stress yourselves. We'll see where the night takes us."

I almost choke on my words, and Summer bursts out laughing. "Really, I don't mind. I kind of miss having him around, and I'm sure my mum can tolerate him for one night this week. Thanks for inviting us. Really. You were great."

Jackson leads Summer out of the venue, snaking an arm around her waist and leaving me and Amber alone at the table.

"I guess I'll be sleeping over on Friday."

"You don't have to," I stammer, letting those nerves creep into my voice again. "I think Summer just wants Jackson to come home to her—no matter what state he's in."

"I think it'll be fun. Although, you have a way of being completely unexpected, so I guess we'll see what happens."

"What do you mean?" I ask, curious.

"I mean...there's something about that pink hair of yours, Ingrid. Since you dyed it, you've been a completely different person. It's like you're growing into yourself. I kind of love it."

"Thanks. I think?"

"Oh, it's definitely a compliment," she says. "Every time I think I've got you understood, you go and do something completely unexpected. You keep me on my toes. So who knows how Friday will end up? Either way, I'm sure we'll have fun."

"Oh, trust me," I tell her, putting every ounce of flirtation I have into the next three words. I want to be confident; I want to flirt. "We'll have fun."

Chapter Nine

"Is this some kind of an excuse to get me out on a date?" Kat questions me, with an amused glint in her eyes. "Because you could just ask, you know."

I laugh loudly, adjusting my dress in the mirror. "Don't be stupid. I just want to have fun."

I turn away from the mirror to face Kat. "What about Amber?" she asks carefully. "I know...uh, I know how you feel about her. If that's still a thing."

"It's still a thing. But, really, Kat. I just want to have fun. As a group. We went to so much trouble getting these fake IDs. We may as well make the most of them, right?"

"Right," Kat answers bluntly, downing the rest of her drink in one gulp. "Jesus, remind me to never let you mix the drinks again because that was ridiculously strong."

"It's not my fault I can handle it better than you."

"Handle it?" She scoffs. "That's one creative way of putting it, I guess. So...are you staying with me again tonight?"

I hesitate, taking a deep breath. "Actually...I invited Amber to come and crash here. We're going to let Jackson go home to Summer; I think it will make her feel better about him going out drinking while she stays at home."

"If she was so worried about that, she probably should have used a condom," Kat mutters.

My eyes widen in shock at her sharp comment. "Jesus, you don't need to be a bitch about it," I snap, feeling immediately defensive of Summer. "What's your problem?"

"Nothing." Kat shakes her head, swallowing hard. "I'm sorry. The alcohol just isn't hitting the spot right now. Is it okay if I go outside to smoke?"

I shrug, not bothering to answer her before turning back to start on my makeup. I don't know what got under her skin, but right now, it doesn't matter. If Kat wants to be moody, then so be it. I'm going to do my best to make the most of tonight—whatever it holds for me.

I smother my eyes in smoky eyeshadow, deciding to let my makeup stand out tonight. I've opted for a simple navy dress with a low back and slim-fitting body. I've spent so much time worrying what people think about me that I've forgotten what *I* like to wear and how *I* like to wear my makeup. This new beginning, this new opportunity for me to grow into my skin, has opened so many doors for me. There were so many things I held back—not just my sexuality. My true opinions, my style, my confidence... It's all coming out now.

I spend twenty minutes focusing on my makeup and sipping my drink. I do not want to be as sloppy as I was last time. At some point, I realise Kat has snuck back into the room and is sitting on the bed silently, watching me intently.

"Jesus," I mutter when I finally notice her. "How long have you been sitting there?"

"A while," she says, obviously stoned. "Sorry for being a bitch."

I turn my attention back to applying the finishing touches to my eyeliner. "Why did you say it then?" I ask. "Obviously, you have a problem with Summer."

"I don't." I can see the genuine regret flashing in Kat's grey eyes. "I'm just PMSing, I dunno. I needed a smoke. I'm better now."

I raise my eyebrows. "I hope so. Come on, we'll have a good night— not for us, but for Jackson. He needs to have some fun. We should probably get going soon; he'll be waiting for us outside the club. I think he and Leon were getting ready together—they're on the same soccer team."

Kat nods absent-mindedly. "And Amber?"

"She'll meet us there too. She has a lot of friends that go to Cloud Nine."

"But I'm sure they'll disappear as soon as *you* get there..."

I roll my eyes. "Okay, Miss PMS. Whatever. Just finish your drink and let's go."

Kat remains silent as we take the short trip on the bus to town. I let her sulk while I stare out the window, nervously twining my hands in my lap. I need to stop overthinking things and just relax. I just want to see where this night takes me. I'm sick of worrying and stressing and wondering. Amber is a human, just like I am.

We get off the bus to find Leon and Jackson laughing hysterically outside the club. It's obvious that Jackson is hammered. Leon meets my gaze, grinning casually. He opens his palms for a hug, and I return it happily.

"You look great," he murmurs. "But I'll let you concentrate on your girl tonight, hey?"

I look up at him, shooting him a grateful smile. "No hard feelings?"

He snorts and I roll my eyes. "No, Ingrid, no hard feelings. Not tonight, anyway."

I smack him on the shoulder and turn to Jackson. He sways on the spot and his eyes are glazed over—but he's standing on his own, so I guess that's a good sign.

"Are you doing all right over there, Jackson?" I smirk.

He grins sheepishly. "I'm doing great. Let's get in and find your lover."

I ignore the anxiety that emerges by Jackson's stupid joke. He knows better than that, but do I trust him to keep his drunk mouth shut around Amber?

"How about you and Kat go and dance off some of that alcohol and Leon and I will get some drinks?" I ask as we head into the club, nodding once at Buster the bouncer. Jackson's eyes are as wide as saucers as we enter Cloud Nine, and I realise that this is probably the first time he's ever been here. I imagine what I looked like on my first night entering this crazy club—that has kind of become "the norm" for me now...

That is, if anything in my life were actually normal.

Kat grins at Jackson and throws me a smirk before leading him out onto the dance floor. To his credit, Jackson walks straight past the topless dancers and begins doing the robot in the middle of the crowd. The men in muscle shirts watch him curiously, eyeing his dorky dance moves appraisingly.

"Let's hope his admirers don't get wind that he's a baby daddy." Leon chuckles from beside me. "They'll eat that right up."

I groan, trying to dismiss the image out of my head. I don't doubt that Jackson will remain absolutely faithful to Summer tonight—he just needs to let off some steam, that's all.

"Come on. I'm too sober for this. Can you see Amber anywhere?"

"You mean, my competition?" Leon winks, leading me to the bar. "Yeah, she's doing shots with the bartender."

My head whips around, and I try to find her through the crowd of people. Leon laughs and points to the corner of the bar where, sure enough, Amber leans forward, taking shots with TJ. She is bouncing enthusiastically with the beat of the music.

"Hey, you," I say as we approach her. "Looks like you've had a bit of a head start."

"A little bit." She hiccups, leaning into me as Leon orders our drinks. "I wanted to make sure I was ready to get on your level."

"My level?" I ask, taking in her simple makeup and flowing grey dress. Her thigh-high boots tap against the metal of the bar, and I can almost feel her energy from here. "It looks like you're ready to dance."

"Oh, Ingrid, I am!" she sings, pressing her body into mine. "Come and dance with me, *please*?"

I am smiling too much. I feel like a lunatic as a tipsy Amber attempts to engage me in what looks like a drunken version of the nutbush dance. I can't help the swelling of admiration as I watch her, the delicious nerves that rattle through me every time I meet her eyes.

"I will. I will," I reassure her. "Just let me grab a drink first, okay? Jackson and Kat are on the dance floor if you want to get out there already."

I am suddenly frozen as she snakes her arms around my waist, letting her legs tangle in mine as we lean against the bar. I can't breathe when she's this close to me, and I love it. Her hair brushes against the bare skin on my shoulders, and I shiver at the feeling.

"I'm staying with you," she murmurs huskily into my ear. "There's no way I'm letting you run off with Leon again." Leon raises his eyebrows at her as he passes me a drink, amused. "No offence, Leon," she adds.

"None taken." He smirks. "You have good taste, I see."

"Taste has nothing to do with it," she says, her voice muffled as she rests her head on my shoulder. "I just want to have fun with my friend, that's all."

I bite my lip, refusing to meet Leon's eyes as I down the shot and quickly begin to sip my cocktail. Goddamn, if I thought this girl was confusing when she was sober, apparently I had no idea what I was getting myself into when she's drunk.

After the bubbles begin to pop in my head and I sway unconsciously with the music, I decide it must be time to dance. Amber squeals with delight and grips my hand as we get onto the dance floor. Leon still tries to catch my gaze, maybe silently trying to ask what the hell I'm getting myself into with this girl.

If only I knew.

Jackson seems a little more put together now, but he still pumps out those classic—and ridiculous—dance moves. He seems to have an audience, following him as he attempts to match the "Thriller" dance with this dubstep beat. Somehow, he seems to make it work.

Even Kat seems to have calmed down a little as she zones in on Leon, grinding against him and swirling in his arms. It appears Kat can't do anything that isn't sexual, and I can understand that now. She's a very sexual person. As the DJ screams at us to drop low, Kat takes it lower than anyone else. Spreading her legs and shaking her butt until it's almost touching the club floor.

Beside me, Amber is twisting and contorting her body as she tries to dance. For someone who is such a great singer and so musically minded, Amber is the worst dancer I've ever seen. I'm thankful for holding back a little on the drinks so I can capture this memory of her attempting to match Kat's slutty dance skills.

Kat disappears for a while, leaving me to wrangle Jackson and Amber while Leon's attention is captured by a petite blonde girl. Jackson beams from ear to ear as he belts out the lyrics, fist-pumping the air and stomping the ground.

When Kat returns, she is stumbling a little, unable to focus on my face. I roll my eyes and pull her close to me, dancing with her until she is stable enough to dance on her own. Amber still twirls mindlessly through the people, laughing as she attempts to match their dance moves, looking like a blind chicken while she does it.

"Let's ditch them," Kat slurs, her voice right next to my ear. "Go back to mine. You know you want to."

I hesitate, pulling away to look her in the eye. She takes the opportunity to close the space between us so our foreheads are touching. My mind flashes back to just a week ago, when I couldn't resist closing the space between us. Do I still want that?

Yes...

"I made plans with Amber." I sigh. "I'm sorry."

She presses her body into mine, firmly gripping my waist as she moves seductively with the beat. "Let her go home with Leon," she murmurs, her lips moving just centimetres away from mine. "He'll look after her."

She lets out a shuddery breath before taking away my opportunity to reply. Within seconds, her lips are gently caressing mine, teasing them with a question as she flicks her tongue between them. The metal stud in her tongue is cold as ice—probably from the cocktail she just downed—and it sends flutters of arousal cascading through my body.

I pull away gently, slipping my fingers behind her neck reassuringly. "Kat...no," I breathe. "I'm sorry. I've got to go home."

Kat jerks away as if I've slapped her, drunkenly stumbling away until our bodies are no longer touching at all. "Really?" she yells, causing Amber and Jackson to stare at us with wide eyes. "*Really*? That's how you're going to play it."

"I'm not playing anything," I argue, putting my hands up in the universal sign of surrender. I don't want to fight with her—not about this. Not here. "Kat, I'm sorry."

"You know, I actually fucking liked you," she spits. "I know. Pathetic, right? I held off for *so fucking long* and then...you get me hooked. You catch me with your giggle and your innocence and your goddamn passion. I should've known better. I should've stayed the hell away from you." She slurs her words, but the anger in her eyes is real. My heart pounds. I don't know what to say—I don't even know how I feel anymore.

Before I can even respond, Kat storms off the dance floor and Leon pulls away from his blonde girl to chase after her. The club still pounds around us, and the music thunders in my ears. Suddenly, it's too loud. There are too many people. No one took much notice of our little scene, but I can't seem to catch my breath. I need to get out of here. I need to be away from this. I need the silence.

Sensing my distress, Jackson wraps a reassuring arm around my shoulders whilst linking his free arm through Amber's.

"And, I think that puts a premature end to our night. Look, guys, I think we should get home," he says, leading us off the dance floor. "There's only so much drama we can take, and Ingrid looks like she's about to have some kind of fit."

Amber is still wide-eyed, probably not trusting her drunk mouth to speak right now. I am thankful that Kat is nowhere to be seen as we exit the club. In fact, the streets are deserted. It's too early for the crying girls and horny boys tonight. All that's left is us—stunned, confused, and desperate to go home.

I'm silent during the taxi ride home. I haven't said a word since Kat's outburst. I thought coming out—coming to terms with my sexuality—would make things clear for me. I revelled in that clarity. I was being true to myself. I was allowing myself to be free.

I just feel more confused than ever now. Kat *likes* me. Summer once tried to tell me that a drunk mind spoke our sober thoughts, and I thought that was just her way of justifying her late-night hookups with Jackson, but I'm starting to wonder if my best friend was onto something.

Beside me, Amber lets out drunken sighs. Her teeth chatter as if we are suddenly in the middle of Antarctica—probably another side effect of her drinking. She catches me watching her and flops her head against the back seat of the taxi, smiling at me.

She jerks her arm out, clumsily finding my fingers in the seat between us. She slips her fingers through mine with ease.

"I had fun tonight, Ingrid," she breathes.

I'm still watching her, watching the night lights hit her face as we get closer to my house. Her hair is wild around her shoulders, and her makeup is slightly smeared from her wild dancing.

She looks incredible.

"I always have fun with you," I tell her.

The silence settles between us, as we sit in the back of the taxi, clasping hands and curiously watching each other. She studies my face intently, as if it holds her life answers, chewing at her bottom lip.

Too soon, we are in front of my house. We stumble out of the taxi, giggling as the driver tells us to take a hot shower. Mum and Dad are heavy sleepers, but I don't know if even they can sleep through Amber's uncontrollable giggles. Before we collapse through my front door, I rest my hands heavily on Amber's shoulders, meeting her eyes.

"We have to be quiet, okay? They can't know we were drinking."

Amber grins sheepishly, letting out a feeble *shh* before nodding firmly. Without giving her any more opportunity to wake my parents up,

I quickly let her through the front door and usher her into my bedroom. I'm not thinking about the way my stomach drops when Amber collapses onto my bed as if it were her own, or the realisation that she has nowhere else to sleep—and nothing to wear.

I just follow her to the bed, gently settling down next to her. She giggles as she lifts her bare legs into the air, kicking them feebly.

"Ingrid," she gasps, wheezing with laughter. "Ingrid, help. I can't get my shoes off."

I let out a chuckle and kneel onto the ground while she pulls herself into a sitting position on the bed. Her boots are laced up past her knees, so there is no chance of kicking them off.

"I'm going to undo the straps and laces, okay? But you have to be quiet." She looks down at me, and a flicker of nerves flash behind her wide brown eyes. Impulsively, I add, "No funny business, okay?"

Her little giggle makes my pathetic joke worth it.

I slip my shaking fingers under the leather of her boot, near the top of her thighs. She squirms and giggles. Her warm skin is immediately covered in goose bumps under my touch. *Jesus.* I need to do this as quickly as my shaking hands will let me. I manage to get halfway down before she starts squirming again.

"Mmm," she murmurs, moving her legs against my hands. "That feels nice."

"Be quiet." My voice shakes almost as much as my hands, and if someone asks me my name in this moment, I probably wouldn't be able to tell them. All I can focus on is getting her shoes off before I do something stupid.

We're just friends. That's all she wants—that's all she'll ever want.

That thought slams into my consciousness with enough aggression to help me unbuckle her shoes without incident. I press my lips together, trying to ignore the waves of confusion that crash through me. I am friends with her. That's all I ever wanted.

She collapses onto the bed, curling into the middle. "Cuddle me," she whispers in the darkness.

My room doesn't feel dark anymore. In fact, I feel like I can see everything. Every smudge of makeup on her delicate cheeks, every curl in her wild hair, every crumple in her little grey dress. Getting impatient with me, she pulls my arms around her, entangling our legs together.

I squeeze my eyes shut, willing for these feelings to disappear. I would give anything to be content being curled up next to this girl, but tonight has not been my friend and feelings are not fair. Her heartbeat thumps against my hand, and I let it soothe me. Tonight, I realise that with truth comes loss. With truth, comes risk and rejection. She is my truth, but tonight, my truth is a sad one.

In finding my freedom, I have found my pain.

Chapter Ten

I SHEEPISHLY AVOID Amber's gaze when we wake the next morning. At some point through the night, she's moved to the other side of the bed, and her eyes flicker open, then grow wider when she realises where she is.

"Morning," she says hoarsely, her voice thick. If I thought her hair was wild last night, it's absolutely crazy this morning. It surrounds her cheekbones in wild ringlets and falls in a pile of fluff around her shoulders.

"Hi," I breathe. My voice is shallow, full of the nerves that were mysteriously absent last night, full of remorse. I don't know what to do anymore—I don't know what happens for me next.

What even happened last night?

"Well, you're gonna have to walk me through last night's events." Amber sighs, pulling herself into a sitting position. Her dress is falling off her shoulders, and she crosses her arms across her chest. "Did we make out?"

The question catches me off guard, and I attempt to analyse Amber's question. Is she hopeful? Does she care? Is she disgusted? Last night, I got absolutely no vibes that she wanted to be near me like that at all.

God, I wish the answer was yes.

"No." I laugh huskily, feeling the effects of last night's drinking catching up with me. "You were pretty smashed, but we danced a lot. Kat and I had a fight, which ended the night pretty quickly. Uneventful, really."

Amber grins. "Damn, I'll have to try harder next time."

I raise my eyebrows. *What is this girl playing at?*

"Maybe you will," I throw back. "I guess the next big party will be the wedding."

"I guess it will." Amber sighs. "I like hanging out with you, Ingrid. I'm happy we're friends."

"I'm happy too," I murmur. "Really."

A comfortable silence settles between us, and Amber sleepily watches me. "Kat's in love with you," she announces. "The way she looks at you, you can tell how much she cares."

I jerk back as if Amber slapped me. This is the last thing I want to hear. This is the last thing I want to talk about. I don't know where I stand with Kat anymore. I don't know what happens next. Right now, I'm just trying to figure things out with the unbelievably beautiful girl sitting in front of me.

This is the girl I want.

It's that thought that sends cascades of clarity settling through me. It's like everything is suddenly in high definition, I'm starting to see everything clearly. *This* is what's important. *This* is what matters. Why *shouldn't* I give things a shot with Amber? Even if it turns out she doesn't like me—or doesn't like girls at all—at least I'll know I tried. Right now, I have nothing to lose.

I owe it to myself. I owe it to Amber. This is something that I need to do.

"Maybe she is..." I relent. "But I'm not in love with her."

"No?"

"I do, uh...I do have feelings for someone, though," I admit, shaking my head, my heart pounding. Am I really doing this? I've come so far. I learnt so much. I have to take the plunge, take the risk. I want her to know how I feel. With the truth comes the risk. It's worth it—I need to be free.

"Who?" She presses her full lips together, her brown eyes wide with curiosity.

She must know. She *has to*. I can't deny that I have some issues with subtlety and, as Jackson so delicately puts it, leering. She must have some kind of clue. After everything that's happened over the past few months.

She can't be clueless.

"Look, it's something I've been thinking about for a while. It's what made me come to terms with how I feel about...girls. It's hard with Kat because her feelings aren't returned. These feelings I have...they make me stumble over the words and act like a bit of an idiot. They make me crazy and excited and...absolutely enthralled."

"Why won't you tell me who it is? I get it. You're in love with someone. But *who*? Oh Jesus, is it Summer? I can see how that would be an issue."

In true Amber style, she is absolutely oblivious and completely off the mark, but as she rambles away, a smile slips across my face. I beam at her. I can't help it.

"It's you. Amber. It's you."

It's like the world stops. My heart stops beating and my stomach drops. The anxiety lifts off my shoulders, and my breathing is easier. The heavy weight of secrets, of trying to push this away for *so* many years, of pushing Amber away...it's done. It's over. This is it.

Our gazes lock on each other, and for a fleeting moment, I wonder if she is going to kiss me. Her eyes are wide, and her mouth has dropped into a perfect *O*. The silence is freeing. I embrace this moment of confession, freedom. I no longer have to hold this weight inside of me for a second longer.

Suddenly, tears spill over, splattering across her pale cheeks. Her breath hisses out in a short gasp that shudders through her body. She wrings her hands in her lap and pinches at each finger as my moment shatters.

"I have to go," she gasps, pushing past me.

And then, she's gone.

I DON'T HAVE the energy to draw. I hardly have the energy to *breathe* right now. As the sobs pound through my body and the rain lashes against the window, the sky cries with me.

I am alone in my misery as I gasp for air, attempting to swallow my sobs. I can't differentiate between the pain of Amber's rejection and the blissful relief of getting this secret off my chest. I needed to tell her.

It was for the best.

That thought doesn't ease the pain that rips through me, as my hands grip the bed railing and my tears don't cease. The sting of this rejection and the ache of this realisation sends waves of pain crashing through my body.

"Come on." Jackson storms into my bedroom, and I whirl around, hastily wiping my eyes—not that it'll do much good. "You need to get out of here. I get it. You're cut up. But a week of misery is enough. Let's get out of here."

"Where are we going?" I ask, my voice cracking with emotion.

"It doesn't matter." Jackson shrugs. "I'm going to cheer you up, no matter what it takes."

I shake my head. "Jackson, I don't want—"

"It doesn't matter," he interrupts, dragging me to my feet. He pulls me into a hug, holding me tight. "I'm sorry that it didn't go how you want it to," he whispers in my ear. "You're an amazing girl, Ingrid. You're going to find someone just as amazing. Someone who lights up your world. Now, put some jeans on. I'm driving."

For a moment, I want to shove Jackson away, tell him to fuck off and let me deal with my own problems. But his kind smile and comforting touch make me reconsider. I need to stop pushing people away. This is a time for forgiveness, for growth, for learning to be okay.

"Fine," I mutter. Jackson looks away while I pull on some decent clothes, using the time to properly wipe my eyes and pull my hair into a messy bun on the top of my head. "Where are we going?"

Jackson turns around, a sly smirk on his face. "That's a surprise."

In the car, the music pounds through my veins. Jackson catches me staring out the window, watching the rain batter against the glass, and turns the music up louder. It's therapeutic; it's everything I need right now. I don't even notice as the town of Port Macquarie slips away from us. Flashes of buildings and gloomy footpaths are replaced with stretches of moss-green forest with dark woods and empty roads. I drag my finger across the foggy window of the car, drawing meaningless shapes as my town disappears through the clear patches of glass.

"How long are we going to drive for?" I ask impatiently. "You're not planning on kidnapping and murdering me, are you?"

Jackson snorts, keeping his eyes on the road. "We're almost there."

If he wanted to take my mind off Amber, he's been successful, at least. I can't dwell on her reaction. I just wanted to give her the truth and she let me. That's all I could ever have asked for. The truth will set you free eventually...even if it feels like hot pokers exploding in your chest.

Finally, after what seems like hours, Jackson pulls the car over into a small gravel car park. I stare around me, with absolutely no idea where we are. We are on a small gravel road, surrounded by bright-green shrubbery and huge trees.

"What are we doing? To be honest, I thought we were just gonna get some food and have a little car therapy session—you've always been good at that kind of stuff."

"Ingrid Harper, you are lost. In your mind, in your art, in your love. So, I'm going to get you lost physically. Come on, the trees will block out most of the rain. Let's go for a walk."

My eyebrows fly up. Obviously, he doesn't know me very well if he thinks that I am going to do any kind of exercise. But I stare out of the foggy car window as the wind violently whips through the trees, as the rain lashes against the windows. Maybe I do need to be out there.

Maybe I do need to get lost.

"Fine." I sigh. "Only for you, Jacks."

WE STAND IN the middle of this muddy clearing as the rain pours down, soaking us through to the bone. The wind howls through the trees, threatening to crack their strong limbs, to crack through the air.

We are miniscule in comparison to the nature that thunders around us. We are covered in mud, panting and lifting our tongues out to the rain, desperate for a little more water.

"Do you feel lost yet?" Jackson gasps through the rain. His smile is huge, despite his flushed cheeks and the dark blond hair that's plastered to his forehead.

"This is incredible," I say, staring up at the sky in awe. There's moss growing on the uneven rocky path, and my tennis shoes are black from the mud. Bruises are forming on my shins from the countless times I've slipped on the forest floor, and my jeans are torn at the knees.

"Do you feel better?" he asks gently.

I lift my hands in the air, feeling the power of the rain against my palms, letting the wind empower me. This is strength. This is beauty. "A little." I sigh. "I'm sorry for the breakdowns. I guess I haven't been the greatest company over the past week."

"Hey, at least it's given me a bit of an idea about what I'm going to be dealing with in fifteen or sixteen years." Jackson shrugs. "I can only hope that my daughter has a smidgen of the strength you have, Ingrid. Seriously."

I nod, reaching out to pat his shoulder. "Thank you. For *everything*."

Jackson wraps me into a sweaty, muddy, wet hug, and I let him squeeze my shoulders, feeling his genuine respect and compassion. "I'm here for you, you know. You opened your house to me. You've helped me and Summer throughout this whole pregnancy. You inspired me to continue with my art."

He pulls away, staring at me, an unyielding smile tugging at the corners of his lips. I feel lost in the moment—of friendship, of strength, of nature's storm. The storm that rages above us matches the storm crashing inside of me. I am nature's storm. I am powerful and terrifying and full of rage and sorrow and anger and passion.

"Come to the wedding. I know Summer is acting a little crazy lately, but it would mean the world to her. Surprise her. Make her night."

Jackson laughs. "You know, I can see right through you. You just want more backup for when you have to face Amber."

I roll my eyes, not amused at being caught out.

"Of course I'll do it. I understand how you're feeling, and I'm going to be here for you. But, if I were you, I'd be more worried about facing Kat. If you thought that *you* were struggling with rejection..."

"Why?" I haven't seen Kat since that crazy night, and I've been glad for the separation.

"She's dyed her hair black," Jackson tells me. "I don't know what it is with you girls and the need to dye your hair every time something crazy happens. She's just...dull. She used to be kind of sexy and mysterious— don't tell Summer I said that—but now she's just kind of depressed."

"Love hurts." I shrug. I don't know where I stand with Kat—I don't even know what I *want* anymore—but I can relate to her pain, and it sucks. I just can't comprehend the fact that she actually *liked* me.

Is it because I feel like I'm not lovable?

"That it does," Jackson agrees. "You'll figure it out."

I shrug, feeling unbelievably small in this massive forest. I'm just a part of nature, a piece of irrelevant furniture in nature's playground.

"Do you think it'll ever be okay? Will I ever figure out this whole lesbian agenda?"

Jackson snorts. "There's no rulebook on this whole lesbian thing. I guess you just kind of get thrown in the deep end. If you want my opinion, though, I think you're doing pretty damn well. Look at you! You're fierce and free. You're living your truth. You admitted your feelings. That's scary. It takes guts."

I nod, feeling empowered by Jackson's surprisingly encouraging speech. Somehow, he knew exactly what I needed today.

That's what friendship is about.

I STARE AT the letter addressed to my mum and dad. It didn't take long for me to whisk it away before they even laid their eyes on it. Thankfully, they were too distracted to notice the very intimidating letter addressed to them that is stamped from my school. Jackson is curled up on the couch, intently staring at his sketchbook as he creates a new comic strip. He's been entering some competitions and putting his work out at school.

Once I'm in the safety of my bedroom, I unfold the crumpled envelope with trembling hands. *This isn't good news.* My gut instinct tells me that this is going to impact me—and not in a good way. Why is it only addressed to them?

My curiosity gets the better of me, and I tear the letter open with shaking fingers. The red letters send cold tendrils of dread dripping through my stomach, and my breath catches in my throat.

As you know, Ingrid has applied for the RMIT scholarship... I bite down hard on my lip as I attempt to comprehend these sentences. *I was contacted by them for a character reference. Unfortunately, I just don't feel that she is up to par when it comes to her theory and grades. I have seen improvement over the last six months... It's just not good enough.*

I throw the letter onto my bed and let my head fall against my bedroom door with a dull thud. I can't read anymore; it makes me sick to my stomach. I want to tear the letter into shreds. I want to burn it with the fire that is igniting inside of me. I want to kick the door down and smash my paint tins against the wall.

Instead, I calmly sit on my bed, taking shallow breaths as I attempt to comprehend the meaning of this infuriating letter. My art teacher. She never said that RMIT rejected me, only that she didn't provide a character reference.

If they wanted a character reference... That means I'm in the running, right? I still have a chance, right?

I snatch the letter back in my hands, reading intently as I attempt to calm my thundering heart. I still have a chance. She was just letting my parents know how shit she thinks I am—I can deal with that. I don't care what she thinks of me. I care what RMIT think of me.

Without a second thought, I scrunch the letter up and kick it under my desk. My passion for RMIT, to get this scholarship and succeed has been reignited. I *will* do this. I can do this.

I open up my sketchbook and begin doodling, attempting to take my mind off that letter and my thoughtless teacher. How dare she completely throw away this opportunity for me? She could've just been honest with them; she could've told them about my improvements lately. I *want* to try. I want to show her that I can be better.

I also kind of want to punch her in the face.

Angry reds and calming blues splatter across the page of my sketchbook as I draw thoughtlessly, attempting to calm my jittering nerves and angry mind. I fall into my art. I become enthralled in the vibrant shades and hollow outlines. I draw without abandon, forgetting about self-editing and the pursuit for perfection. Right now, my urge to draw and create is taking over all of the negative emotions that have been weighing me down over the past week.

I let go of my thoughtless teacher and the rocky path that will be my future career. I push away the uncertainty and the fears of not being good enough.

In this moment, my art motivates me; it soothes me and give me strength. I let it heal me. As I draw, I become calm. I am at peace about Amber's reaction. I can't hold it against her, and I can't allow it to taint any chance of having a friendship with her. Any connection with her is better than not having her in my life at all. She is something special, and when you find something special, you do everything you can to keep those people in your life—even if it causes you pain for a little while.

Eventually, I will move forward. I will fall for someone else—someone who returns my feelings. I will find love and acceptance and peace. It will all happen. It doesn't have to happen tomorrow, or anytime soon, but it will someday.

Chapter Eleven

"THANKS FOR STAYING with me tonight," Summer says again, collapsing onto her bed.

I shrug, sitting down next to her. "It meant that Jackson could have my bed for the night, so I think he was appreciative of that. Besides, we need a game plan for your mum's wedding this Saturday."

Summer rests her hand on her stomach, and I admire her bump for a moment and how with her arms she instinctively protects the baby inside of her already. "I guess I probably should've paid a little more attention to things when it comes to the other side of the family." She hesitates for a moment, watching me carefully. "How do you feel about...seeing Amber?"

I sigh. This conversation was inevitable, and Summer's done well to dance around the subject up until now. I know that she is inherently curious about every single detail of what happened with Amber, since all I've told her is the basics, but she's watching out for me and I appreciate that.

"Look...I don't know what happened that morning. It's like, I finally had the guts to tell her and...I got nothing. No resolve, nothing. Just rejection."

"Well, it wasn't really a rejection," Summer attempts to reassure me.

"I told her I had feelings for her, and she left crying. I think that's pretty clear," I say harshly, trying to drop the bitter tone from my voice. "The problem is that this is one of those times where turning to alcohol would be great, but I need to stay sober enough to walk you down the aisle—that's assuming you still want me to?"

"Of course I want you to. And, during the past five and a half months, I've learnt that alcohol doesn't really fix any problems—in fact, from what I see, it kind of causes more. I watch you guys drinking and hung-over the next day. I watch all of the drama it causes, and..." She looks down at her stomach thoughtfully. "I'm so thankful for my little bean. I would stay home in my pyjamas every single night for her, and it's worth every minute." She looks up at me, and I nod at her to continue. "So many people told me that being a teen parent would be the end of my life—no drinking, no more being selfish, no school...but I can't imagine anything different, Ingrid. I can't imagine my life going any other way anymore. *She* is my life. She's everything."

"You don't wonder what would happen if you hadn't gotten pregnant?" I'm not scared to ask Summer the difficult questions—in fact, I love that about our friendship. She challenges me just as much as I challenge her. We question each other's reality; we make each other look into things just that little bit deeper.

"I know how they would've gone!" Summer answers. "I would be getting drunk with you every weekend, probably breaking up with Jackson every *other* weekend, and I'd still be useless at school and have no university prospects at all."

I beam at her as she happily contemplates her future.

"Look, I don't *know* what happens next for me. What I do know is that I'm going to love this little girl with everything I've got. I will be an amazing mum, and I am going to work to give her everything she could possibly need. That's what I know."

I shake my head, trying to suppress the wave of emotions that crashes inside of me. Summer being so determined is making me want to cry, and as my eyesight grows bleary, I realise that I've become way too in touch with my emotions recently to suppress them anymore.

"Goddamn," I groan, wiping the tears that splatter onto my cheeks. "Look what you've done now."

Summer launches over to my side of the bed, wraps her arms around me, and holds me tight in the nook of her shoulder. "I always knew you had a heart." She giggles. "I'm sorry. I want you to know that you're the one who has given me strength, Ingrid. You helped me see the power that I had within me and that everything would be okay. *You* did that."

Through my tears, I smile at her. "Thank you. You're going to be amazing, Summer. You already are."

She pulls away, shaking her head and wiping her own eyes. "Oh my god, you're setting me off now. Come on. Let's talk about the wedding again. I'm sick of being a hormonal crying machine."

I take a second to compose myself, turning my thoughts to the wedding. I've been avoiding thinking about it for so long, but I'm going to have to face Amber. It's inevitable. "I guess, I just have to compose myself. I want to be her friend. I really do. I would rather be her friend and feel the way I do than be nothing at all."

"But wouldn't that just kill you?" Summer asks, throwing one of those particularly hard questions at me. "If you had to be friends with her, holding on to these feelings? I know it would kill me."

I bite my lip as I consider her question, mulling over the thought of having to face her, to spend time with her. "I guess I'm kind of used to it." I shrug. "The difference is, now I can be myself—my *true* self. I can live my life, and I'll move on from her eventually. It doesn't mean that I want to shut off all possibilities of a friendship with her, you know?"

"I know," Summer says. "I get it, I guess. But I won't leave your side! So, you don't have to deal with any awkward alone time."

"I wouldn't mind being alone with her," I ponder. "Just for little bit. Maybe it will give her a chance to explain her reaction."

"Well, I won't go far," Summer insists. "Oh hey, on the plus side, my dress still fits! Looks like baby girl decided to be kind to Mama and not grow ten inches this month."

"Hey, you've still got five days to go." I wink. "Don't speak too soon."

As I walk into the school courtyard, feeling thrilled with the cool breeze that tickles the hair hanging near my shoulders, Kat sits alone at a table in the corner. I think it's the first time I've ever seen her alone at school before, and I take a deep breath, deciding that now is as good a time as any to clear the air with her.

Today, the sun is high up in the sky with not a cloud in sight. It's the kind of day that makes you appreciate everything we have in this crazy little world. I know that my short floral dress is completely mismatched with my rough army boots and wild pink hair, but with this weather, I don't really care.

Kat tears up a cigarette box, pouring all of her concentration into ripping up the fragile cardboard. She's so enthralled that she doesn't notice me approaching until I am sitting next to her. She looks up, and her expression is frozen, her lips are pressed into a tight line.

"Hi."

"Hi," she responds.

"I, uh...I wanted to talk about the other night..." I begin nervously, twining my hands in my lap. "I guess I was pretty drunk, and I really didn't give you much of an opportunity to say your piece."

"I'm surprised you even want to talk to me." She raises her eyebrows, surprised.

"Of course I do," I assure her. "Look, we've become pretty great friends over the past few months, and I don't want to give that up over some drunken fight. I want to hear what you have to say without a bunch of sweaty people bumping into us and music pounding over our heads. I thought, with the sun shining and the courtyard is quiet, we've got a full hour to talk things out, so why not?"

"That's assuming I want to talk about it."

"You do," I tell her. "I know you do."

Her cool façade shatters, and she lets out a small laugh. "Of course, I do. I fucking *hate* letting things fester. I just want to get it all out in the open and move on as quickly as possible."

"Go ahead then." I nod, turning my full attention to her.

Kat takes a deep breath, turning her gaze to the chipped woodwork of the table. "Look..." she begins. "When I first asked you to come to Cloud Nine, I honestly was just messing with you. I saw the new pink hair and you were strutting around, and I thought...*yeah, I'm gonna put her in her place. She needs to get an attitude on her.*" Kat pauses, grinning at me, and I return her smile, feeling amused. "I never thought you'd actually say yes. But of course, now I see how bloody stubborn you are, that you never really realised what you were saying yes to, did you?"

"No, I didn't care."

"I think you did care a little bit. I get now that you were looking to try something new, and I suppose I kind of helped you come to terms with everything." Her smile is radiating, and I want to wrap her into a hug because it's true. She really did help me.

"I never expected to actually...like hanging out with you."

"I like hanging out with you," I say. "Seriously, I have so much fun with you, Kat. I hate that the other night got ruined."

Kat hesitates, chewing her lip as she picks at the chipped woodwork on the table. "I guess...I guess I let my guard down a little. I don't *do* that, Ingrid. I don't let people in. It's just…you were so oblivious and nervous that I never thought about *my* feelings. I was always thinking about your feelings. Then…things kind of got out of control, I guess."

"What do you mean?"

"That night…the night that we hooked up, I started to listen to my feelings. I started to realise that…I like you, Ingrid." Kat avoids my gaze. "I've liked you for a while now."

I am picking at my chipped nail polish, suddenly feeling ultraaware of everything happening around us. The sun still beams down on us, and the courtyard is still full of people shouting and laughing. There's still the incessant buzz of the school's announcement system…but all I can concentrate on is Kat and the way she is sitting next to me, looking so vulnerable.

My stomach is clenched, and my heart is in my throat because I don't know how I feel, I don't know what to say. I don't know why I thought she would say anything different because, deep down, I *knew* that she felt this way.

"I shouldn't have gone home with Amber the other night," I mumble. "I should've stayed with you."

Kat looks up sharply, a sceptical expression flashing across her face. "I shouldn't have been so crazy. I don't know why I suddenly felt the need to scream at you across the dance floor. Like, what? That's not me. I'm sorry. Really. It was a shitty position to put you in, and I don't expect you to say anything about it."

"No," I argue. "You're allowed to feel that way. I'm…I'm kind of jealous because I *wish* I could tell you what's going through my mind. But nothing makes sense anymore."

I bite my lip, trying to stop the emotion from pouring out with my words. Kat is putting everything out there right now and being completely honest with me. I don't need to take that away from her by being overdramatic.

"Did anything happen with Amber?" she asks quietly.

I shake my head, my eyes flickering shut as I try to suppress the memories of the other night. I don't want to go back to that moment. I have to focus on moving forward and seeing her on Saturday.

"I told her the truth, and she made it pretty clear that she would never feel the same way," I choke out. "I should've known better."

Kat reaches out, hesitantly placing a comforting hand on my thigh. "It's the straight girl curse," she says. "I should've warned you about that."

I laugh a little. "Yeah, you should've. Are there any other lesbian problems you need to warn me about?"

Kat sighs, pulls her hand away, and leans away from the table, staring out into the courtyard. "Yeah. I should warn you how much more it hurts when they *do* like girls but they don't like you..."

Chapter Twelve

THERE ARE FAIRY lights strung across the trees, and they twinkle in the twilight. The blood-red sunset illuminates the beautiful field, full of lush greenery and exploding with bright-yellow sunflowers. The soft lilt of the acoustic music drifts across the field, melting into the forest that surrounds us. As the sun falls into the cloudless pink abyss, it melts across the grass and highlights the faces of the people watching the ceremony.

I stand beside Summer as she watches her mum. Her hair falls into light-brown tendrils around her shoulders, and her tan skin looks stunning in this golden hour. Her hands are clasped around her bump, holding a fresh bouquet of yellow daisies. In the audience, Jackson's attention is glued to Summer, and the smile that dances radiantly across his lips is infectious. There is only love in his eyes.

Amber sits in the audience too, but I don't let my eyes linger on her for too long. She watches her uncle with a face of pure joy. Her hair is an explosion of tight ringlets around her shoulders. There's glitter on her eyes and a beautiful peach colour on her lips. If her gaze flickers to me, I don't notice because I am trying so hard not to look at her.

The ceremony is short and beautiful. Summer begins to relax and embrace her mum's new relationship as we get closer to the reception. As the sky finally dips down behind the trees, the couple enjoy their first kiss as husband and wife and the audience explodes into applause.

Summer and I follow them down the aisle with our arms linked, laughing as the overdramatic music carries across the field, and we make our way to the reception area. I head straight to the bar, deciding that that's probably the only way I'm going to be able to calm my vibrating nerves with Amber around.

"Do you wish you could drink right now?" I ask Summer as I sip on my bubbly champagne.

Summer shakes her head vigorously, turning to watch the audience streaming out of the chairs and into the reception area. I can tell she's looking for Jackson—there is nothing but love for him.

"I wouldn't change it for the world. The vomit, the fear, the money...it's all worth it. And besides, I don't need alcohol to enjoy this."

"You're right, this place is beautiful," I agree. "And the ceremony was nice."

"It was," Summer answers distractedly as she locks gazes with Jackson, who makes a beeline straight towards us. "Let's just hope this one sticks."

"I have a feeling it will. Hey, you're related to Amber now."

"Awesome." She rolls her eyes. "Hey, babe, you look great."

I turn my attention back to the crowd that are making their way into the reception area while Jackson and Summer are being cutesy. My thoughts are straying to Kat and our conversation in the courtyard. I wish I could have her confidence; she is just so calm within herself. Even with her new black hair, she is still so...*Kat*. She is just uniquely herself.

I sigh and down the rest of my champagne before turning to the bartender for another. As I do, someone taps me on my shoulder. I'm silently willing for it to be anyone but Amber. I could deal with anyone but her.

Unfortunately, life is not that kind, and Amber's full lips smile back at me.

"Hey," I choke out, quickly grabbing the plastic cup from the bartender.

"Hey, I have to do my set in half an hour, but can we quickly go somewhere to talk?"

I turn to Summer for help, but she is suddenly too interested in her conversation with Jackson to even notice me at all. "Okay," I say quietly, then follow her as she walks towards the secluded area of the forest by the stage.

We sit on a creaking little bench, and I admire at the entwining flower chain of daffodils that runs across the stage. I can't imagine how long it must've taken someone to make that chain, but the daffodils appear to be real because they are beginning to wilt already.

"Look, I just wanted to say sorry for the other morning." Amber launches into it straight away. "I shouldn't have—"

"Hey," I interrupt her, shaking my head. "You don't need to apologise. I should've kept my mouth shut. We were hung-over, and honestly, I should've seen the signs. End of story."

"No, Ingrid..." Amber sighs. "*Stop.* Stop trying to be so tough, stop trying to put words in my mouth. I shouldn't have left you like that. I should've listened to you and...that's what I want to do right now. I want you to tell me again how you feel, Ingrid." Amber takes in a shuddering breath. "Give me another chance to hear you."

Her teeth graze over her bottom lip, and she keeps glancing towards the edge of the stage as if she's worried that we're going to run out of time or something.

"Why?" I ask, narrowing my eyes. "So I can embarrass myself again? So you can run away crying again? Or do you have another plan?"

The suspicion that bubbles up inside of me feels like acid. It feels like anger and vulnerability. I don't want to be afraid of Amber. I want things to just go back to normal. I want to be drunk in the back of a taxi, watching each other quietly and holding hands. I want *that* back.

"No, no!" Amber says hurriedly. There are bright red splotches melting across her pale cheeks. "I just want to listen to you. Please..."

"Look, there's nothing left to tell you," I tell her abruptly. "I told you everything."

Amber hesitates. "Did you? Because I feel like you really didn't tell me anything. How long have you had these feelings? Where did they come from? Was it before or after you realised you liked girls?"

"It doesn't matter." I frown. "You don't feel the same. I need to move on."

"*Please.*"

I pause as the desperation flashes behind Amber's huge eyes. For whatever reason, she is asking me to take a leap of faith. I think about Kat sitting in the courtyard with me and being so startlingly honest with me. I admired her courage. In that moment, it didn't matter how I felt because she was letting the honesty set her free. How I feel doesn't matter.

I take a deep breath, firmly telling myself that this is for Amber. If I want to salvage any kind of friendship with her—and I most definitely do—then I should tell her the truth. I should let my honesty set me free.

"It's something I've felt for a long time," I begin, then take a nervous breath in an attempt to calm myself. "I didn't realise it and...I guess that's why I was such a bitch to you." I frown. "I hated you because of how you made me feel. I hated everything about you. But...I also loved it," I choke out, blinking back tears. "Because you made me *think*. You challenged me. You made me realise that there is more to life than just dull make out sessions with lame guys that don't lead to anything. There is more than feeling like nothing is good enough, like nothing made me excited."

Amber stares at me, eyes wide. I meet her gaze nervously as I compose myself.

"It started with watching you sing," I continue, wringing my hands together. My whole body trembles and my voice shakes, but I push forward. "And then suddenly I knew your uploading schedule, and I couldn't help but watch your videos. Obviously, you know that I would come to watch you perform." I try to laugh, but it's lodged in my throat. A small smile flickers at the edge of her lips, but it doesn't go further. "And...that's it." I shrug. "I was falling for you. I started coming to terms with everything, and it was because of you. I totally understand that you don't feel the same, but...the other night, I guess I hoped you did."

Amber's eyes shine as she watches me, her hands clasped in her lap. She fights back tears, and it pushes me over the edge. I wipe my leaking eyes, not caring about smudged makeup or looking like an idiot. Right now, the emotion is real, and all I can do is watch her trying not to fall apart as I fall apart in front of her.

There are people beginning to get up on stage, and her gaze flickers towards them. "I have to sing now. But I want to continue this conversation. It's not over."

She gets up, smoothes out her dress, and takes a deep breath. I stand up too, putting a hand on her shoulder. "It is over." I sniff. "It was never beginning."

Amber shakes her head, pulling away from me. "It's not over," she tells me.

I STAND AT the back of the crowd as Amber sings. Summer and Jackson are on the dance floor with Summer's family, leaning on each other as they dance slowly to Amber's romantic, lilting lyrics. The sun has fallen behind the trees, and the marshmallow sky has been masked by inky streaks almost as black as Kat's new hair. The fairy lights that are twined through the trees and along this field twinkle in the moonlight, swaying softly in the summer night breeze.

Amber tries to catch my gaze during her performance. It's something I had hoped to happen for so long, something that would make my heart leap at the possibility. The hope that she was singing to me. Now, I just want to bury myself behind this bar and drown in this champagne. She sings softly, letting the atmosphere for the bride and groom become soft and loving.

Other couples dance with each other. Some, like Jackson and Summer, are content with holding each other and swaying to the music, occasionally leaning up for a kiss or a secret whisper. They are the couples that stare into each other's eyes, not daring to look away—not even for a second. There are other couples who twirl and bow and—in the case of Summer's drunken aunt—*leap*. They laugh and fall into the music and let it take control of their bodies. It reminds me of how we dance at the club—without hesitation, without fear. Letting the music lead our bodies, letting ourselves go.

Amber sways with the music as she huskily sings the lyrics of this little love song. Her voice is like a soft sigh, letting the audience in on a secret. Although my cheeks are still burning from my earlier confession and I don't dare meet her eyes, I am still mesmerised by the way she sings. I always will be.

As Amber sings, I don't notice that Summer has broken away from Jackson until she is making her way through the dance floor towards me. I finish the rest of my drink quickly and walk to meet her halfway.

"This mama needs to sit down." She grins. "Will you take over with Jackson? He's enjoying dancing."

"I don't think that would be appropriate—slow dancing with your baby daddy!"

Summer rolls her eyes. "Of course, it would be appropriate. Now get out there before he starts trying to dance with my mum."

I shrug and find Jackson in between the kissing couples and swaying dancers. He breaks into a smile when he sees me and opens his arms for me. "I knew Summer wouldn't just leave me high and dry. Would you care to dance, m'lady?"

"Well, I'm sure the bartender would appreciate a break from me." I chuckle, wrapping my arm around his shoulder. I rest my head against the crook of his neck, and we begin to sway to the music.

The acoustics are so much better down here on the dance floor, and Amber's voice surrounds me. It lilts through the air, softly settling around me, giving me shivers. I close my eyes and fall into the music, feeling comforted by Jackson's warm body against mine.

"You really love her, don't you?" His breath is hot against my ear.

I look up, confused. Out of the corner of my eye, Amber watches us as she sings. The song is reaching the climax, and her voice grows louder. She reaches into the air as if bringing her strength to continue with the lyrics.

"I guess I do," I mumble. "It doesn't matter, though. She doesn't feel the same."

"Then why has she been watching you all night?" Jackson murmurs, stroking my bare back with his fingers. "Seriously, if her eyes were a mirror, they would just be reflecting wild pink hair and your risqué little black dress. That's it. No one else is getting any attention from her tonight."

I roll my eyes, and Jackson brings his hand up to a much more acceptable position on my back. I know better than to think he's flirting with me. Old habits die hard, and I will always be comfortable in Jackson's presence. He is my safe place.

"Have you thought of any names yet?" I ask, bringing the subject back to something that I know Jackson will be more than happy to talk about.

Jackson shakes his head and a smile dances across his lips. "Not yet, but we have some ideas. It just makes it so much more real now that we can say we're having a girl. I'm gonna have a daughter."

"You are." I nod. "And you better damn well raise her to be a strong independent woman."

Jackson laughs. "Between you and Summer, I don't think she'll have anything to worry about."

"I think you're right."

The silence settles between us, and we sway slowly as the crescendo builds and Amber's beautiful voice seems to shatter around us. I'm lost in it, as I dance with Jackson. He quietly leads the way, letting me follow him as we dance slowly.

Around us, people are whispering and watching Amber in awe. I know that I'm not the only one who appreciates her music. It is husky and strong as it builds up slowly, only to come crashing down around us just seconds later.

Summer watches us from her position at the table, eating a piece of bread and smiling. I know that she's happy to see me having fun with Jackson, and to be completely honest with myself, I'm just happy that they are happy. I don't ask Jackson about the screaming fight he was having with his dad on the phone the other day or mention that Summer has been missing class and her grades are quickly slipping. They know this. They know the challenges that are up against them, the fact that the world is spinning on a different axis than they are, and that they are going to have to grow up more in the next four months than they will in their entire life.

I dance slowly with Jackson, as the music swirls around us and Amber's voice vibrates through my body. We grip each other's hand. Right now, nothing matters but this dance, this moment, this decision. I came clean to Amber. I smoothed things over with Kat.

I've got this life thing down. I'm doing okay.

As Amber sings and, for the first time ever, I show my appreciation by dancing along, I allow myself to enjoy the moment.

"Thanks," he breathes in my ear, giving me my own sweet little whisper. I wasn't jealous of the happy couples that dance around us, but it's nice to know that I have my own little whisper buddy. "For always keeping me grounded."

I can't help but laugh, and I pull him closer to me, giving him a reassuring squeeze.

"Trust me, you're the one keeping *me* grounded. Always."

Jackson and I dance for the remainder of Amber's set. She switches from slow, contemporary, husky ballads to upbeat, hopeful love songs filled with trembling notes and wavering lyrics.

She captures the attention of the crowd, building them up with her promising lyrics and then crashing them down. We are at her mercy with her beautiful performance, and I can't help but fall into her voice.

Afterwards, Jackson and I wander over to Summer. She's still smiling at us as she eats her second helping of bread. "Are you gonna go and talk to her?" She grins, raising her eyebrows. "Or did you get everything out before her performance?"

"She said she still wants to talk. Speaking of which, I need another drink. Jackson, want one?"

Jackson snorts before shaking his head. "I think I'm done for the night."

I shrug and head towards the bar. I'm not drunk yet, but I don't know what to expect with my conversation with Amber. Already she's managed to catch me off guard tonight.

The bartender hands me a glass of champagne before I even have to ask—he already knows what I need. I give him a wry grin and drink quickly as Amber speaks to her band members with a huge smile on her face. The adrenaline that a performance like that gives her is obvious. She is radiant by the end of it.

As she exits the stage, she walks directly towards me. Before turning to me, she gets a drink as well and sips quickly.

"That was awesome," she breathes. There's a light sheen of sweat highlighting her features. Her lipstick is a little smudged, and her hair is wilder than it was before.

"It was," I agree. "You were great."

It feels good to acknowledge her talent, instead of lurking at the back of the room or watching her videos intently. I held my tongue for so long, hiding my appreciation for her. I hated it—I wanted her to know how much of an impact she had on me.

"Let's get another drink and go for a walk," she says. I notice that she gives me no option to say no.

When she decides she wants to do something, she makes it happen. That's Amber.

We get our drinks and wander behind the stage. I can feel Summer and Jackson watching us, whispering to each other. I ignore them and walk with Amber, escaping the rowdy crowd.

We walk in silence for a while, looking up at the glittering fairy lights and sipping our drinks from their plastic cups.

"I'm sorry if I freaked you out before." I sigh, finally breaking the silence. "I shouldn't get so emotional about these things. It's just...I'm not like Kat and I can't just be cool no matter what."

"Do you like her?" Amber asks quietly, not looking at me. She becomes very interested in ripping up her empty plastic cup.

I laugh, trying not to be rude in my surprise. "Are you serious? We're talking about my feelings for you and that's what you're wondering?"

Amber shrugs, lifting her gaze to meet mine. She looks concerned. "I just know that you guys have become close. I don't want her taking advantage of you. That's all."

She sounds so defensive as she mumbles the rest of her comment. I stare at her in disbelief. We stop walking, and I realise that we are alone in a dark enclave of the forest. The twinkling fairy lights are bright in the distance, but alone in this field, we are surrounded by the inky black sky.

"You can't be serious," I say, crushing my own plastic cup in my hands. I attempt to keep my voice calm as I turn to face her. "That's the last thing she would do, and honestly, I can't believe you would say that."

She drops the plastic cup onto the grass—I don't bother asking if she is planning on picking it up because I know Amber better than that and *of course* she is—and she takes a jerky step towards me.

"So you do like her."

The swellings of frustration begin to burn in my stomach, and I try to quash them, letting my confusion take over. "What is your problem? I spent the last forty-five minutes before your performance telling you how I feel. Why are you asking about Kat?"

Amber blinks quickly and seems to relax a little, gaining some perspective from my comments. "I don't know," she mumbles. "I just don't understand it."

"And I don't understand you," I respond. "That doesn't mean I need to question you about it."

"You're right..." she says slowly. "Why don't you question me about it? Not once have you asked about how I feel about you."

Her cheeks are flushed red, and a bad jazz band starts up at the reception, filling the void of silence that has sunken between us.

"Because it's *obvious*," I insist. "Jesus, it's like you just want to reject me over and over again. I don't understand why you need to keep pushing this. You know that I want to be friends with you, and that can't happen if you insist on embarrassing me and rejecting me."

"How do you know that I'm going to reject you?" Amber snaps back.

This question catches me off guard, and I pause for a moment, trying to build up the courage to answer her. I'm sick of giving her the answers that I think she wants to hear. I *need* to be more like Kat. I need to be honest.

"Because if you weren't going to reject me, you would've made a move by now," I retort. "You have always loved the attention, and this is something extra special. Well, that's it. It's done now. Congratulations on ruining any chance of a friendship between us."

Without waiting for her response, I bend down to pick up her cup and turn to storm towards the reception area as fast as my shaking legs will take me. Amber grabs my arm and rips the cups out of my hands, throwing them to the ground.

She pulls me towards her, roughly bringing my hands to her waist. She throws her arms around my shoulders, staring me in the eyes. Her hazel eyes are huge and blazing, and her lips are slightly parted, letting out short gasps.

"Kiss me," she demands.

"No!"

"Why not?" Her grip remains strong around my shoulders, and I notice a flash of disappointment in her eyes—I've ruined her dramatic moment, it seems.

"Because you *don't want me to*," I hiss. "You just want the attention."

"Oh forget it," she mutters, quickly closing the space between us. Before I can register what is happening, her soft lips crash against mine, and the moment isn't soft like I imagined but full of anger and confusion and passion.

I let out a gasp as her tongue slips between my lips and her body strains hard against mine. Her fingers entangle in my hair and her lips move with purpose. Hesitantly, I trail my fingers along her waist and fall into this violent kiss. Amber is determined, as she pushes my head closer to hers, tugging at the back of my body. It sends thrills cascading through my skin, dancing carelessly across my arms. I can't catch my breath as she traces the outline of my body with her determined fingers.

I want nothing more than to drag her closer to me and deepen this moment, to thrust my tongue into her mouth and graze my teeth across her voluptuous lips. I want to feel her body shatter in my hands, to feel her determination as I take control of the kiss.

Instead, I drag myself away from her wandering hands, and with more effort that I've ever had to put into anything in my entire life, I pull away from the kiss. For a moment, we stand frozen, staring at each other with wide eyes. She gasps for breath, and her lips are pink and puffy from the kiss. The red splotches on her cheeks have melted across her neck and chest, and her hair is tangled around her shoulders.

"Why did you do that?" I gasp.

Amber stares at me. When I throw my question at her, her eyes flicker shut as if I've hit her. Her chest heaves and her hands are frozen in front of her.

"I just wanted to know what it was like," she stammers. "I-I just wanted to try it."

"*You* wanted to *try it*?" I screech with disbelief, like Amber is clenching my heart in her fist. "What? I'm just an experiment? You don't feel the same way! Why the hell would you do that?"

I can't quite catch my breath, and the startled expression flashing across her face like lightning sends tendrils of doubt into my stomach. I don't want to think the worst of her. I don't want to be defensive. I want to believe that she is like me—confused. But her wide eyes and pursed lips tell me that there is something more.

"I just thought it would be something to try," she backtracks. "You were up for it. I'm sorry if you thought it meant something else."

"I'm not your experiment!" I spit, desperately trying to stop the swelling of hurt exploding into my voice. "You knew how I felt."

"Does it make you like me more?"

Since I've known her, Amber has been the most dramatic girl in the room—in the *world*, probably. She lives for the drama, for the attention. She has chewed up the reputations of boys and spit them out mercilessly, claimed to fall in love with gay boys, claimed to be cheated on, claimed to be alone, to be the victim...

I never thought she'd be like that with me.

What fascinated me the most about Amber was the deeper side of her—the side that I could only ever catch glimpses of. A deeper side, a vulnerable side. She was something special, something to be figured out. I strived to understand her.

"So, that's it?" I demand. "It was just for the attention? You don't actually care about me?"

My mind spins, and as the fairy lights twinkle through the leaves and the breeze tickles the hair around my shoulders, I realise that Amber has played her game. To her, I was just another dramatic montage, another thing to check of her list.

Get a lesbian to fall in love with me and rip her heart out? Check.

Kiss a girl? Check.

That's it. Her life is just a checklist. I *know* this. I've watched it happen, I've watched her go through this checklist over and over again; I've watched her cause drama so she can write a song, or have some gossip, or use the anger to get out another YouTube video.

She uses people.

"You knew how I felt," she mumbles, avoiding my gaze. Her hands now writhe against each other in front of her stomach. She nervously yanks at the material of her silk dress. "I just wanted to see what happened if we kissed. That's it. I'm sorry."

I spin around, desperate for her not to see me crack. I don't want her to see my expression crumble or my trembling lip or the tears that suddenly spill down my cheeks. My legs shake, and I will myself to hold it together—just for the next five minutes.

"Fine," I throw back at her. "You've had your fun. Now get the hell out of my life."

Chapter Thirteen

ART.

I hide in it. Paint-splattered jeans, with reds and greens and purples. Inky fingers that turn grey from blue and black ink. It is in my hair, on my clothes, on my face. The paint covers me; it protects me. I am a part of the art. I *am* the art.

The art room is my sanctuary. No one bothers to speak to me. The music from my headphones is on a constant blast—so loud that it can probably be heard from a different room. I drown in it. It pulses through me as I protect myself, as I rebuild the walls that I worked so hard to tear down.

There are storms and forests and mountains. Landscapes filled with beauty and chaos and sheer impossibility. There are crashing waves and roaring lions. Wilting flowers and blooming weeds. I am nothing. I am everything.

I hide in my creations. I ignore the compliments and the criticisms. I am my art. I am alone. I don't want feedback or support or advice. I do not need anyone else, just my paintbrush and this blank canvas in front of me.

The looming results for the scholarship applications motivate me. I grow determined. I consider the worst and the best situations—what could happen and what is more probable.

I breathe heavily as I through my my latest creations, feeling the adrenaline hammering through my body. It vibrates across my paint-stained skin. I look like a canvas myself. I'm covered in colours and splatters of all shapes and sizes. I can feel it drying on my face, coating my hands. I don't care. I am in the art.

This art comes so naturally; it is a part of me. It explodes from within me, crashing and cascading until I can't fight it anymore.

The art is my safe place. It keeps me from breaking down, from destroying every ounce of hope and self-confidence that has grown inside of me over the past four months. I promise to be kinder to myself, not to hate myself. In my art, I seal my promise. I grow as the paintings take shape in front of me.

With each painting, I am going in blind. I don't know what I will see until it is finished. I don't plan on anything. My inspiration takes me where I need to go. My anger, my frustration, my pain, my empowerment...controls my fingers as I drag them across the canvas. I let it create from within.

Sometimes, I can feel Kat's gaze on me. As she sits quietly in the back of the room, staring at her sketchbook, I can feel her curiosity burning into me. She doesn't ask questions. She doesn't speak to me. When I walk into the classroom, she averts her gaze. When I paint, she watches me. When she draws, I watch her. We don't watch each other. We don't let our curious eyes meet. I don't try to speak to her.

I don't speak to anyone.

Jackson tries to strike up conversation, inviting me to lunch and to Summer's ultrasounds. He accepts my silence as my decline. I can't let myself shatter. I have to build up those walls. I have to be strong.

Accepting my sexuality tore me open like a gaping hole in an already fragile bed sheet. I was vulnerable, I was open. I became thin, fragile. I let myself be ripped away, destroyed. I shouldn't have gotten close to her. I never should have told her how I felt.

I can't live with regret.

But I can't live with the fact that Amber Freeman used me, just like she uses everyone else. I can't accept that there was never anything deeper. Those glimpses that I caught, the promise of something deeper, the quiet, fragile part of her that had me burning with curiosity, aching to know more about her...it was all a lie.

She shouldn't be a singer. She should be an actress.

At that thought, a bitter chuckle escapes my lips and my finger slips, splattering a deep black gash across the green forest on my canvas. At that moment, I realise I'm going crazy.

I need to talk to someone.

I need Summer.

"THAT BITCH."

I nod grimly as Summer stares at me in disbelief, sitting across from me on my bed. I didn't cry when telling her what happened, and I consider that my achievement for the day. My room is a mess of unfinished canvases, torn sketchbooks, and crumpled poster paper. There are open paint bottles strewn across my desk, leaking their beauty across the dark woodgrain.

"I should've known." I sigh. "Actually, you're my best friend—you should've bloody warned me. There's nothing more. She's just as dramatic and manipulative as she ever was. When people show you who they are, you have to believe them."

Summer hesitates, picking at a loose cotton thread on my bedcover. "I thought she was different too. Did I think she was a lesbian? I don't know. But I thought she was at least a decent person."

"I did too. I guess I just let my feelings get in the way."

Summer strokes her stomach absent-mindedly. Her bump is huge now. She can't wear any of her old clothes and, for the most part, just wears Jackson's shirts. Somehow she still manages to look great whilst doing it. The girl has style.

"Oh well, onto the next." She shrugs, making the bold statement in a way that only Summer can. "Do you think something will happen with you and Kat?"

I shake my head vigorously. "If the past week has taught me anything, it's that I need to get my mind off girls. I need a game plan to figure out what I do if I don't get into RMIT. That bitch teacher probably ruined all my chances."

Summer raises her eyebrows sceptically. "No offence, honey, but if I'd just come out with my love for boys, the last thing I'd be doing is staying away from them. You need to get out there and explore your options."

I snort at her bold assumptions, and she purses her lips defensively.

"As for your art, I will support you one hundred percent. I mean, I'm not going to lie and tell you that you are definitely going to get into RMIT because that letter was horrible. But you have talent and you're going to go far. I know that for sure."

I tug at the ends of my pink hair, tearing the split ends away, admiring the pink hue. As Summer carefully tiptoes around my future, I find myself facing the hard truth—I have no idea what I'm doing.

"Goddamn, I wish we could drink together." I sigh.

Summer snorts. "Speaking of this little beauty, I need to ask you a favour."

I hesitate. Summer's favours lately have been slightly questionable. From three in the morning pickle deliveries, to faking doctor's notes to get her out of coming to class, to answering the phone when the school tries to call her parents. I know that Summer is strong, but I can also see when she is struggling. She doesn't ask for help—she disguises it in meaningless "favours" that help her get through the week.

"What is it?"

"I need you to go house-hunting with Jackson," she answers hurriedly. "I can't stand being around my mum and Mark anymore, and we really want to move out before the baby comes."

"Oh." I shrug. "Yeah, that's fine. Why can't you go?"

"That brings me to my next favour..." she says slowly, squeezing her eyes shut and clutching her stomach. She's not playing the cutesy pouting game anymore, so I can see this one is serious.

"Yes?"

"I need you to move out with us." She rips her eyes open and stares at me, fear masking her dark features. "We can't afford to do it on our own. We need you there."

I hesitate, considering the possibility of living with Summer and Jackson—and, eventually, a newborn baby. I hadn't considered moving out until I knew about the results of my scholarship application. I'd never considered living with Summer and Jackson, even though I've practically been living with Jackson for the last two months.

"Jeez, way to put a girl on the spot," I mutter, looking up at Summer. "Look, you know I'd love to—even with the baby. But what about money? What about a job?"

"I know, I know," Summer says. "It's going to be hard. We'll all probably need to get jobs. Please just say yes!"

I laugh a little, because I know that if I said no, Summer wouldn't push me. The truth is, I don't want to say no. I'd love to live with her. "I don't even know what I'm eating for dinner, let alone what I'm doing in the next six months. But I would love to live with you guys. If we can make it happen, I'll do it."

Summer breaks into a smile. "We'll make it happen," she says with determination. "We can do it."

I'm fighting the scepticism that bubbles inside of me, I want to believe that we can do it. "What if I get into RMIT?"

"Then we'll all go! I'd be happy to live in Melbourne! I'd be the hottest young mum there. Seriously, though, if that happens, we'll make it work. You'd be able to help Jackson get motivated with his art. There are a lot of job opportunities there."

"I guess," I allow. "Okay, fine. I'll go apartment-hunting with Jackson, and if we find something we like, we'll go for it."

Summer's face softens. "You don't think you're getting into RMIT, do you?"

I shake my head slowly, fighting the sadness that grows at her question. I'm sick of feeling sad. "I don't think so. It's just a feeling."

"Wow," Jackson forces out. His arms are folded tightly across his chest as we walk into the dingy apartment.

I sigh loudly, fed up with the smirking realtor. We've been at this for an hour now, and every apartment seems to get worse. Her skirt is too tight and her heels are too high, and if I had to tie my hair in that tight of a bun, I'd go blind.

In this particular apartment, the walls are mouldy, the floor creaks, and it has a funky smell. I roll my eyes as the realtor begins listing all of the "amazing" benefits of this horrible place.

"And of course, it's very cost-friendly," she says stiffly, watching Jackson carefully as he paces through the tiny lounge area.

I suppress a groan and follow Jackson into the bedrooms, feeling more frustrated with every second that passes.

"This is a waste of time," I mutter. "Let's go."

Jackson shakes his head as he turns to face me, his eyes wide with desperation. "I want to find the perfect place. For us. We need to keep looking."

I place a comforting arm on his shoulder. "Jackson, this is useless. She's just showing us crack dens now. There is no way I'm letting any of us live in a place like this. We'll look online. Let's get out of here."

"Do you even want to live with us?" he snaps, dragging a hand through his messy black hair. There are bags under his eyes, and the stress pinches at the corners of his lips.

"Of course," I answer. "But that bitch of a realtor isn't making this search any easier. *Let's go.*"

"Excuse me?"

I whirl around to see the snide realtor staring at us with her hands on her hips and her nose in the air.

Great.

"I said, we're outta here. Ciao."

I grab a gobsmacked Jackson by the arm, and we run out of the apartment, falling against each other as we burst through the front door and onto the street. By the time we get out of there, Jackson is wheezing with laughter, and my heart swells to see him happy.

"Forget about her," I tell him. "Let's go get some eggs benedict and figure this out. We're gonna find the right place, but she was a bitch. I want this to be right for all of us."

Jackson nods and begins leading the way to the little café on the corner of the street. I follow him inside and we sit down, still breathless from the laughter.

"Have you thought of any names for the baby?" I ask, after we order.

Jackson shakes his head. "We can't agree on anything," he says with amusement. "You don't realise how many people you hate until it's time to name your baby. We'll figure something out."

"I heard Ingrid is a pretty good name." I wink.

He chuckles and grips his coffee with both hands. "I'll consider it a possibility." He grins. Then his expression softens and he hesitates before saying, "Summer told me you don't think you're getting into RMIT. Is that why you agreed to move in with us?"

I shake my head vigorously. "I guess she forgot to mention that if I *did* get into RMIT, that I'd be dragging you both to Melbourne with me, but, no, I don't think so."

"You're an amazing artist, Ingrid," Jackson murmurs. "I saw your scholarship application. You have everything going for you."

"Except that damn letter," I mutter.

"I mean, that's not the greatest, no," Jackson allows. "Still, you've got a chance."

"You never applied. Why?"

Jackson shrugs, staring down at his coffee. "That's not really the path I want to go down—even if Summer hadn't gotten pregnant. I guess I'm kind of realising now that I don't need a degree to know that I love to draw."

I stare at him in awe, wondering why I'd never considered that before. Why *did* I apply to RMIT? I've never been interested in following the "traditional" route in life—married with three kids and a green Volvo. It's just not my style. So, why did I think that university was the only option? I don't need to be validated when it comes to my art. I know that I've got talent. I know that I want to make art and make money. I *can* do that—I don't need some stupid school to teach me how to do it.

"I guess you're right." I frown. "I never thought of it like that."

Jackson grins at me. "I'm good at making you think, aren't I?" He smirks. "I've always had that effect on you."

"You have that effect on *everyone*." I roll my eyes. "You're special like that."

"So, our apartment options were pretty shit." He sighs. "What are we gonna do?"

"We'll figure something out," I say. "We always do. Besides, I think I could really enjoy living with you guys. It might inspire me to actually pay a little more attention to my art—I could have my own little art studio!"

"Whoa, cowboy. You're getting a little carried away there. We can barely afford a two-bedroom apartment. What makes you think we're going to be able to find one with a studio? I can't work extra shifts at some crappy restaurant for the rest of my life. But I do think that we'll inspire each other to do more with our art. Maybe we should start some kind of business? That'll pay the bills."

"A business?" I scoff. "With our art? What are we going to do?"

I want to believe that Jackson has some great idea, something that we could do. But there's nothing. I'm going to end up washing dishes or packing groceries just to pay the rent. I don't want to get stuck on that conveyor belt. I don't want to be forced into a life that I don't want just to live my dreams.

"I don't know. I'll think of something."

The slight spark of determination in his eyes tells me that he *will* think of something. I trust that Jackson's ability to dream big will mean that he'll come up with something. Whether it's possible or not is another question...

"JESUS, INGRID, PULL your damn dress down!"

Leon's booming laughter can be heard even over the pounding club music. It explodes around me as bodies rub against mine, bumping into me. I can't see straight. Bursts of colours blur in front of my eyes, the flashes of light seem to spasm in front of me. I can't quite catch my breath, and I can't even hear myself talk. If I could, I know that I'd be telling Leon to shut up.

I dance in my own world, the alcohol fuelling my movements, my body moving with the music. I can't control my jerky movements, but I sway my hips with the music and throw my arms above me.

Kat dances next to me, grinding against a dark girl with brown hair that frizzes free around her shoulders, beautiful curls exploding from every direction. I stare at her as she grips Kat's waist and realise that I want to kiss her. She's beautiful.

A heavy hand grips my shoulder, and I lean into it, thankful for the rest as the incessant beat wrestles with my exhausted body. I can't seem to focus on anything anymore, and suddenly, my eyes flutter shut. I want to curl up into bed.

"Don't even think about it," a husky voice mutters in my ear. "Let her be happy. You had your fun."

With a heaving breath and what feels like the last of my energy, I spin around, meeting Leon's dark stare.

"I'm lonely," I slur. "Don't wanna be alone."

Leon wraps his arms around me, and we sway with the music. Even though the beat is strong and the relentless pounding doesn't cease, we pretend that the song is slow. Leon curls his hand behind my neck, softly tugging at my hair.

"Kat is not your answer," he breathes. "Just dance."

My mind spins. Actually, the entire room spins. I spin.

The world vibrates and flashes and the bodies pound and there is absolutely nothing stopping me from becoming engulfed in this pounding mess. I am one with the music. I am part of the people. My drunken mind scrambles for some kind of strength, and as I slow dance with Leon, giggling quietly into his shoulder, I find my quiet place.

In the mess of people and music and alcohol, I am just a tiny ant. The sexual frustration is thick in the air, and I can't help but let it seep through my skin, sending urges and loneliness cascading through my body.

"I miss Amber," I mumble.

Leon sighs, gripping my waist and moving his body against mine. We dance for so long that when Kat disappears with the beautiful girl, I don't notice anything except for my gasping breath and vibrating body. I don't want to go home. I don't want to be alone.

I'm sick of being lonely.

"I'M GLAD YOU didn't go home with anyone," Kat says, her voice croaky with exhaustion. She grips her coffee, staring into it as if it holds her life answers, and the bustling café seems to quieten around us when she makes this declaration.

I don't know if it's because I can read a different interpretation to her words or the fact that I really don't know where we stand anymore, but I find myself hesitating. I don't know what to say. I don't know how to answer her.

"I was too drunk." I sigh. "Leon had to call Jackson to come outside and get me. I probably ruined his night."

"If I know anything about Leon, it's that nothing will ruin his night. He probably just went out to keep partying after dropping you off at home."

"I didn't think of that. That makes me feel better."

"That's my job." Kat winks.

"Well, I don't have to worry about wondering if you had a good night. I barely got a glimpse of you before you went off with that girl."

Kat seems to perk up at the mention of her girl. "Yeah, she was stunning. We had fun."

I ignore the pricks of envy that sting across my skin. The realisation that I am completely, utterly lonely has been weighing heavy on me since last night. I woke up alone, feeling even sadder than I did last night. I don't know how to move past this. It's like I've just opened my eyes to all of the possibilities around me, and I've put all of my energy into this one girl.

I need to let go and move on.

"How much fun?" I force my voice to stay level, as I direct my question at her.

"Enough," she answers slyly.

"Maybe I should do that next time. Bring someone home like I did with Leon."

"I mean, Leon wasn't *really* what you wanted, was it? As for taking a girl home, I don't know about that. I've had a bit of practice."

I roll my eyes. "Of course, you have."

"Why? Is that a problem?" she challenges me.

I shake my head, quietly turning back to my coffee. I'm used to Kat challenging me, to her pushing the boundaries and making me think. The truth is, I can't think straight at the moment, and it's got nothing to do with the hangover. I just don't know what I'm doing anymore.

"Kat, this is ridiculous." The frustration edges into my voice. I can't even bring myself to meet her eyes. I just stare into my coffee, inspecting the caramel swirl, studying the white froth the covers the top of it.

"What?" she asks, her tone softening.

She reaches across the table and places a comforting hand on my arm, stroking her fingers across my skin. All I concentrate on is staring at my coffee and composing the whirlwind of emotions exploding within me. I let out a shaking breath, grazing my teeth over my lip.

"How do I move on?" I don't want to cry. I *won't* cry. "Why did she have to kiss me? Why did she have to ruin it?"

Kat is silent for so long that it forces me to look up and meet her eyes. Obviously, that's what she was waiting for because she flashes me a sympathetic smile and tightens her grip on my arm. "Honey, I'm going to have to give you some real talk."

I hesitate. "Okay?" I'm scared. When Kat gives me a warning, it usually means she's going to say something I won't like. We're sitting together in this crowded café, surrounded by mothers bouncing their babies on their laps and businessmen talking loudly on their phones. If what she says upsets me, I can't show it.

Maybe that's what she wants.

"When I first realised I liked girls, it was when I had my tongue down my best friend's throat," Kat begins. "It was our party trick, you see? You know those messy house parties when people are desperate for some kind of entertainment? Something new? Well...we were the entertainment. We'd hooked up *so* many times before this, but for some reason, that night, I wasn't quite drunk enough when she started kissing me. I realised that I enjoyed it. So much more than I enjoyed kissing boys."

I frown at her. I thought Kat liked both boys and girls. Then again, I guess there is no guidebook to sexuality; there is no set of rules or things that we must or must not like.

"And that night, when she finally went off with some guy who'd been ridiculously turned on, I realised that I fucking liked her. I liked her *so* much." Kat takes a nervous breath as she tries to compose herself. Her hand still grips my arm, and she's obviously fighting back emotions as she falls into the memory. "I'd spent so long catering to those boys. I liked turning them on. I wanted them to want us. I spent so long caring about what they thought, stressing about how attractive they found us, that I didn't realise that I was falling for my best friend."

"What happened with her?" What I don't add is that I can tell that this story doesn't have a happy ending. Kat's eyes are still dark.

"Well, I did exactly what you did with Amber. I told her. Why not, you know? I hated feeling those things and not doing anything about them. It went on for a while before I finally plucked up the courage to tell her how I felt, that it was more than just kissing for me. Of course, we were drunk."

"Uh-oh," I mutter.

"She screamed at me." Kat's voice wavers. "God, she was so angry. She said that I was using her, taking advantage of her. She called me a pervert. The thing is...I told her because I *felt* all of those things. It felt wrong making out with her at parties just to get the attention from guys, when I didn't even want their attention. I just wanted her."

"And?"

"And nothing. We stopped being friends. We never really spoke after that. I started hooking up with anyone that took my fancy—guys and girls. And I enjoyed every moment. I stopped caring about what people thought of me. I decided to just do things for me."

"But how did you move on from her?" I ask. "You obviously really liked her."

"The whole screaming-at-me part kind of helped. And, honestly? It took a long time. Longer than I'd care to admit. There is no right way to move on from someone, no specific formula. You just have to do what makes you happy, and happiness will follow."

I smile at my friend, amazed how quickly this friendship has blossomed between us. A year ago, I didn't even know her name. I was an outcast, ostracized from the whole art faculty. I felt suppressed and frustrated and alone. I know that I'm lonely and that this whole Amber thing is going to take time to get over, but I'm not alone. Having people like Kat as my friends means that I will never be alone.

Chapter Fourteen

"SHE'S *OBVIOUSLY* IN love with you," Summer says, as we sit in my car after her doctor's appointment. She's progressing perfectly, and in another two months, she'll have a beautiful baby girl. We don't really talk about the whole birth part—I think she's trying to avoid facing that fact for as long as possible.

"I don't think so," I argue. "Look, what she told me really helped. You've seen me—I haven't cried all week!"

"No, but getting so drunk that my boyfriend has to put you into bed is kind of concerning. Seriously, I think you have a drinking problem."

"Okay, Mum." I roll my eyes. "Look, just because you're about to be a mum doesn't mean you have to start acting like mine. If you keep saying stuff like that, I'm going to tell you all the horrible things I've read about giving birth."

The stricken look that flashes across Summer's face tells me that's the *last* thing she wants to hear about right now. She crosses her arms over her bulging belly protectively.

"Can't I just keep her in there?" she whines. "I just love feeling her little kicks and hiccups all day. Giving birth is fucking terrifying, and it means that I won't be lying down, eating, and just feeling her move all day. It means no sleep and a lot of stress and having cracked nipples and no sex with Jackson."

"Because sex has been on the top of your agenda since you got pregnant?" I snort. "Look, the fact that you're worried about all this stuff—although, probably not the sex—is a good sign. It means you care. You're going to be an amazing mum, I know it."

"As long as I can do a better job than my mother did," Summer mutters.

"You will. I know it."

"I'm scared, Ingrid."

"I know." I sigh. "Look, if it makes you feel better, I'll be in the room when you give birth, okay?"

Summer has been begging me to agree to be in the room with her for weeks now. Actually, from the moment she realised that pooping on the table while she gives birth was a possibility, she was determined to get me in there with her for 'distraction for Jackson,' apparently.

Her face lights up at my agreement, and I'm glad I can take her mind off the fear for a second.

"I've actually been able to get some savings from working with the school nurse," she says, referring to our high school nurses program. "I go there after school and clean the whole damn place, big belly and everything. She even makes me clean the bathrooms—which are disgusting, by the way—but it's worth it. It's the least I can do, really."

"Look, I think the fact that you're going to school *and* doing some work at thirty-two weeks pregnant is enough."

"I guess. Mum actually seems pretty impressed. And, of course, she is completely supportive of us moving out together. I think the thought that she was going to have to deal with a newborn again was more terrifying than the fact that her seventeen-year-old daughter got pregnant. She knows that I can look after myself."

"I think you've made that pretty clear," I agree. "I just wish we could find the perfect place."

We've been looking at apartments almost every week. Everything in our price range is either falling down or completely unsuitable for a child—or it's just a straight-up crack den.

"We will," Summer says determinedly. "I can't wait."

Over the last seven months, I've seen a new side of Summer. There's a new optimism in the way she speaks, in the way looks at the world, making the best of a bad situation. She seems to thrust away the negative energy, ignoring any setbacks that life throws at her, of which there have been many. Summer is special in her strength and persistence. She is exactly what I need in my life, the motivation I need to work towards my dreams, to pursue my art, to become a better version of myself. She truly is the best kind of friend that anyone can have.

Once again, I marvel at the amazing support of the people that have let me stumble into their lives. These kinds of people are so rare, and when we come across them, we have to recognise how lucky we are.

I truly am blessed to have friends like mine.

"I can't believe you're going to have a baby in two months," I say in awe.

I helped Jackson install a car seat into his car last week. It involved a lot of swearing, some bruised fingers, and at least three coffee breaks, but we got there in the end. Even though it's a free day for our grade, Jackson is at school all day, working on the outlines for his comic book series. In between that, he's been applying for jobs both here and in Melbourne. He confided in me that he thinks I will get into RMIT and that he likes the apartments better in Melbourne.

"It could be less than two months," Summer says. "I'm *huge*. I don't know how I could possibly get any bigger. She's going to explode out of me."

"Jackson told me that you guys have thought of a name?" I ask, wincing at the visual.

Summer nods enthusiastically. "We argued for so long. I honestly thought our baby girl was just going to be nameless, but we finally found one that we both agree on. Adeline."

"That's a beautiful name."

"Yeah," Summer agrees. "I'm almost certain that's her name. You know I talk to my stomach? Like, I'm certifiably crazy now, I swear."

"You're not crazy," I disagree. "You're excited." I reach down and pat her bulging stomach, feeling flutters of movement underneath my hand. "Hey, Adeline." I laugh, feeling like a bit of an idiot. "I can't wait to meet you."

I HOLDING THE envelope. The breath has escaped from my chest, and there's a pit of terror weighing down in the bottom of my stomach.

This is it.

My mum wordlessly handed me the envelope as I walked through the door. Her eyes were wide with curiosity, and I knew she was desperate to know the contents. When I told her that I wanted to open it alone, she'd reluctantly accepted it. So, here I am.

With shaking fingers and a heavy breath, I force myself to tear open the envelope. I need to know—I have to get this over with.

I need to figure out what I'm doing with my life.

I scrunch my eyes shut, embracing this last safe moment of uncertainty. Right now, nothing is certain. There is no pressure on me to succeed or make any decisions. In this moment, I don't consider the possibilities or the what-if. I let myself become calm. I wait for my heart to slow and my breathing to become even. I loosen my grip on the paper and open my eyes.

As soon as I open them, the words are there in front of me. My heart falters, and every effort I put into becoming calm just a moment ago fails. Suddenly, I am completely numb. I can't feel the dry paper against my sweaty hands. I can no longer feel the heavy weight on my chest or the incessant pounding of my heart. I am nothing. I am lost as my eyes try to focus on the words in front of me, not daring to accept their stark meaning. *How can I do this?* How can I move past this moment? How can I shake out my frozen limbs and stand up? How do I live my life?

What do I do?

The black ink swirls in my vision, the stark-white paper blinding me. The words are clear, grounded in their undeniable truth. The printed words have determined my future. They have decided everything—they've given me no choice.

This is my truth. This is my future.

I gave them everything I had. I created a piece of artwork for this scholarship that was a raw reflection of me. It was every ounce of my truth and my vulnerability. She was my happiness, my truth, my risk, everything that I couldn't say. She was the beauty and vulnerability and freedom. She was the leap that I took to apply for this scholarship, and she determined my outcome, my future.

As I created my portrait for this application, it made me realise that I was good enough, that I *love* girls. I love art. This application represented all of my growth, my opportunity, my individuality. This application was my hope for a stronger, stable future. It was everything I needed and the only chance I had.

She was everything that I couldn't say, everything that I wanted to scream to the world. She was Amber in her curious flashes of quietness, Kat in her overwhelming confidence, and Summer in her strength. She was me in her uncertainty. She was beautiful and flawed and a part of me. I put everything into creating her for my application. I gave her everything. She was my hope, my chance to get out of this town, my chance to go to a good school.

But she just wasn't good enough.

MORE ALCOHOL. MORE dancing. More kissing.

Who am I kissing?

I don't even know anymore. The cycle of unforgiving club lights and drinks that are far too strong for my worn body. I don't care anymore. I don't want to be conscious, to be aware, to know what happens next.

I don't care what happens next.

This is what I am right now. This is all I can be. Drunk and dancing like a crazy woman in the middle of this crowded club. I don't know how I handled my problems before this, but it doesn't matter right now because all I need is another drink. That will make me feel better.

The sting of my rejection was dulled about three drinks ago, and as I grind against a curvy blonde girl, I realise that I don't care anymore. I didn't want to go to the damn school anyway.

I don't know where my friends are. Did I even come with any friends? The song reaches its climax, and I spin around as the blonde girl grips my ass, pulling me closer to her. She aggressively slips her tongue into my mouth, dragging her lips against my mouth. I gasp and press my body closer to hers, thrusting my hips with the music. My hands slide under the waistband of her jeans, and I loop my fingers around a flimsy G-string. She gasps and thrusts her body against mine. We move with the music, alone in this crowded club.

I don't even know her name.

Do I even know *my own* name?

It's this striking thought that seems to throw me out of my body, and I pull myself away from the nameless blonde girl, then stumble off the dance floor and away from her. I can't do this anymore. My body is numb. I can't feel anything. I can't touch anything. *What am I doing here?*

I bump into people, shove past them as I gasp for air. I need to get out of here. I can hear the blonde girl shouting after me, but I violently shake my head and keep shoving through the crowd.

Someone grabs me by my shoulder, and I wrench it away, staggering through the masses of dancing bodies. I need to be alone. I can't breathe.

I shove past Buster the bouncer, who snorts in my direction, and suddenly I am surrounded by freezing air and the night sky. I sink down into the dark alleyway, my knees scraping against the cold concrete, I'm aware of the tears streaming down my cheeks. They leave freezing tracks from the chilly night air, and my nose is stuffy. I gasp for air as the sobs wrack through my body, and I can't seem to calm my shaking hands.

"Ingrid!"

I jump up unsteadily, my head whipping around at the sound of *her* voice. I would recognise it anywhere. It pierces through the drunken moans and laughter from the people spilling out of the club, and I grip the brick wall behind me as I try to see her through the darkness.

"Amber," I mutter, finally catching sight of her. She bursts through the back entrance of the clubs and storms towards me. Even in my drunken state, her eyes are like fire.

"What the hell are you doing?" she yells, coming to a halt in front of me. I study her as I try to force my inebriated sight to focus on her. Either I'm swaying on the spot or she is swaying in front of me, but I can't seem to get a grip on what she looks like right now.

It's only that deep part of me that inherently knows when Amber is near. Her presence has always ignited a spark from inside my stomach, burning so deep that it fizzles out on my cheeks to let me know that she is close.

"I'm just having fun." The words slur out of my lips in messy, broken tones. My breath falters through my simple sentence, and I rest my head against the brick wall, crossing my arms tightly in front of me as I meet Amber's gaze. "Why are you here?"

Amber squints at me as if she's trying to understand what I'm saying. Her cheeks are flushed, and her stormy eyes are still angry.

"You were embarrassing yourself," she hisses. "Did you even come with anyone? Or are you into drinking alone now?"

I glare at her as I attempt to stop the world from spinning. The dull thump of the club behind us seems to be vibrating through this brick wall, keeping me awake when all I want to do is curl up in bed.

"Why does it matter?" I snap. "Why do you care? Just leave me alone."

My foggy thoughts break through my angry mind, and I try to find the words to tell Amber that I *did* come here with Leon, but he went home with a girl. I wasn't ready to go home. I can't find the words to tell Amber how lonely I feel... Why would she care?

"You need to get a grip. What are you doing to yourself? I want to be your friend. I want to help you, but I can't do that when you're shutting me out."

"Leave me alone!" I shout, as angry reds explode in front of my eyes. "You reject me, RMIT rejects me, just leave me alone."

Suddenly, I'm crying again. The sobs are wracking through my exhausted body, and the tears are streaming down my cheeks. The freezing night air has shocked my system, and my numb body seems to have come screaming to life as Amber's words entice rage from within me.

"RMIT rejected you? I didn't know that."

"It doesn't matter," I spit. "I'm sick of you pretending you care! You fucking kissed me just for fun. You fucked me up! Why did you have to do that?"

"I didn't mean to!" she yells. "I was confused!"

"I hate you," I hiss. "I hate you. I wish I never talked to you. I wish I never met you. Why did you have to do that? Why did you have to make everything worse?"

"I think you're overreacting. You're hurt because of RMIT, not because of me. We were friends."

"We were *never* friends!" I scream. There are other people wandering through the alleyway, drunk and stumbling, laughing loudly. I ignore the heads that turn when I raise my voice; I don't care what they think. I don't care what anyone thinks anymore. "You just wanted the attention. That's all you ever wanted. You don't care about me or my feelings. You don't care about anything except yourself!" I am screaming at her, letting every ounce of my anger and frustration come exploding through my words. "You didn't have to kiss me. You should've said no! You should've said you're not interested. You manipulated me! *Leave me alone!*"

I shove past her with the intention of storming away down through the alleyway. She grabs my arm, and I spin around, my breath coming out in fractured gasps.

"Ingrid, please," she begs. "I want to be friends with you. I do. I shouldn't have done that. I shouldn't have kissed you. I'm sorry."

Her apology sends cold pains stabbing through me, and I just want to break down. Even though my drunken, dramatic mind screams at me to yell at her, to make her feel even an ounce of the pain that is exploding within my chest. I want her to understand how much that kiss ripped everything that made sense out of me and tore it up in front of my eyes. It was half a step forward, one million steps back.

"Just leave me alone," I gasp, wrenching my shoulder out of her grip. "Please."

The tears splatter down my cheeks, leaving frozen tracks in the cool night air. I stumble away from Amber, drunkenly promising myself to let go of the anger.

Chapter Fifteen

THE MUSIC SWIRLS around my ears, calming me, comforting me. I hide in the soft pastels and cool watercolours, letting my brush move against the canvas, flicking and swirling along the white, creating beauty. Soft swirls and sharp lines, blurring into each other and melting onto the canvas, creating unintentional beauty in their existence.

I escape with my playlist, letting the fears, the pain, and the uncertainty melt away into a soft, beautiful painting, allowing myself to fall into the colours—pale pink and soft yellow. Mild greens and melting blues. A field of flowers slowly appears in front of me, tenderly slipping across the stark white of the canvas. My art seeps into my skin, going deeper into my bones, comforting me, giving me the calmness I need. I imagine a soft wind dancing through my hair, touching the blades of grass, and softly caressing the pastel pink flowers. Even though I am inside the art studio at school on this muggy Monday morning, I can feel myself inside this field of flowers. I put myself in this field as I create it, letting myself escape and the world fall away from me.

Right now, I am alone with my music and my canvas. I don't care about RMIT or my fight with Amber. I don't let myself think about what happens next, because I will figure it out. I always do.

All I care about is creating the perfect shadow across this blissful field, all that matters are these delicate flowers and my slow, steady hand as I create a new world in front of my eyes. The music is soft and lilting, gently caressing me, comforting me in the soft strumming of a lone guitar and a haunting voice that sings quietly in my ears.

"Ingrid."

I pull the headphones out, and my peaceful moment comes crashing to the ground as I turn to face the door. My steady hand is frozen in front of the canvas as though I'm scared if I put down this brush, I'll lose that determined slow burn of inspiration inside of me.

Kat leans against the doorway, her arms folded protectively across her chest. Her black hair seems brighter today, and if I look closely, I think I can see the remnants of her old blue streaks. I don't know if it's because of my focus on colours or if I'm finally starting to see the world in it's true, bright reality again.

"Hi," I murmur, finally letting my hand set my paintbrush down on the table beside me. Kat's eyes flutter shut as I say hello, and I don't miss the striking look that crosses her lips. "Are you okay?"

I don't know if it's Kat's demeanour that makes me tense or the residual energy radiating through me from last night's argument, but suddenly, I can't seem to relax. My body is tight and my head feels like it's under pressure.

Kat shakes her head so slightly that I'd miss the movement if I weren't watching her intently. It's now that I'm noticing the dark circles under her eyes, the paleness on her cheeks and the lack of care she's given to her makeup today. Maybe it's the humid weather that's leaving her dry, but my gut tells me that it's something more.

"I saw you last night." Her voice is gravelly and precise as she meets my eyes. "Dancing with that girl? You were off your face. I tried to call out to you after you ran off, but you ignored me."

"I didn't hear you," I correct her instinctively. I don't know why I feel immediately defensive. I shouldn't have to explain myself to anyone. "I was having fun. What's wrong with that? Should I have invited you?"

The snide comment slips out of my lips before I can stop it, and I blame it on the hangover. My temper right now is ridiculously short, and I can't help but let the frustration that's been burning inside of me for weeks now.

Kat's eyebrows rise and her lips purse. "Really?" she snaps. "That's how you're going to be?"

I frown at her. "Sorry. I didn't mean that."

"No, you did," she argues. "You know, I kind of wish I'd never asked you to come to Cloud Nine with me. If it wasn't for me, you'd never know about it and maybe things would be different…"

"How would they be different?" I ask, trying to fight the angry urges inside of me. This isn't me.

Kat shrugs, making no effort to take any further steps into the art room or come any closer to me. "I feel like you're relying on the alcohol." Her voice is so calculated, and she's holding back—which is something so rare for Kat, it makes me uncomfortable. "Like, you need it to deal with everything going on... I know the rejection from RMIT was tough and everything with Amber..."

I frown at her, wondering how she knew about RMIT. Is it really common news that I'm not good enough?

"Drinking and dancing is fun, but it doesn't fix your problems. You can't keep running from things, Ingrid. It's not healthy."

I bite my lip, attempting to hold back my sarcastic comment. Kat watches me intently, and my cheeks burn under her gaze. "Are you saying that as my friend or..." I'm letting angry Ingrid take control of my mouth, and I mentally slap her shut. "Sorry." I sigh, shaking my head. "I don't know what's wrong with me."

For some reason, those words seem to crack inside of me, and I swallow hard, fighting the crash of emotions inside of me. I blink back tears and stare at my feet, trying to compose myself. I don't want her to see me break.

"No, I get it," Kat tells me. Her steps announce she's slowly getting closer to me, but I refuse to look up. I can't trust myself to speak yet. "It's hard... When you feel so alone, you get so lost. How can you trust anyone, when you can't even trust yourself? I get it, Ingrid."

I finally build up enough courage to look at her, and her face is full of compassion. I take a slow breath, searching hard to find the right words.

"What can I do to fix it?" I ask, my voice shaking. "I hate this. I hate myself right now."

Kat reaches out and puts a soft hand on my arm. She is quiet for a moment as she watches me, and I don't let myself fall into the whirlwind of emotions exploding within me. I control my tight lips and taunt body because all I know is control.

Control is all I have right now.

"You can't fix it." Kat sighs. "This is life. You are growing; you are learning. You are going to make mistakes. But I like you, Ingrid, and I'm going to be honest with you because I don't want to see you hurting. As your friend, I am here for you. If you need to yell and scream and rant, I am here. If you just need someone to spend those quiet nights with, I am here. Whatever you need, I am here." Her voice starts to shake and her green eyes shine. "I really think you should hold back a little on the clubbing and alcohol. It stops you from thinking clear, and right now, you definitely need to think clear. You're going through a lot."

For some reason, hearing her say that I'm going through a lot seems to validate my feelings. Like, for so long, I shoved it down. I pretended that my drinking and going to the club was just for fun. But, from the beginning, I was running to escape from my problems. I wanted to ignore everything—Amber, my sexuality, RMIT…everything.

"You're right," I choke out. "I can't keep doing this to myself. It's not fair. I need to sort my head out."

"You do," Kat agrees. "That's okay. That's what I'm here for. Whatever you need, Ingrid, I'm here."

Without thinking, I wrap my arms around her. Her sweet-scented perfume seems waft through the whole room, and I'm comforted by the smell. She pulls me in tight, softly encircling my waist with her hands. I rest my head in the crook of her shoulder.

"Thank you," I breathe. Her skin is covered in goose bumps, and her lips press against my hair. I sigh into her shoulder and tighten my grip.

I want to say so much more. I want to tell her how much it means to me to have someone who understands what I am going through, to have the opportunity to have her in my life. She is more than someone to lean on, more than I can even explain.

I want to say so much, but right now, all I can do is grip onto Kat as tightly as I can.

"I SWEAR TO god, she is going to come exploding through my stomach, tearing her way out," Summer says, staring at her bare stomach in awe.

I'm staring too, wondering how on earth someone so small could've gotten so big in such a short span of time. She traces her fingers along her bulging belly, poking and prodding her skin as if Adeline will come bursting out any second.

"I mean, you are huge." I shrug. "But I feel like that's the last of your problems. You're gonna have a real-life baby in less than a month."

Summer looks up, a huge smile spreading across her full lips. This pregnancy has changed her skin, her face, everything. She looks so different—stunning, but different.

"I can't wait. All of this craziness, this chaos is worth every second. We're going to get through it. Every hard moment will be worth it—even pooping myself when I give birth."

I snort with laughter and so does she.

"But seriously. I know we're still looking for places to live and this next month is going to be crazy, but I just can't wait."

"I'll be sure to remind you of your excitement when you're knee-deep in baby poop and haven't slept for four days straight." I wink.

"It's getting so close," Summer continues. "Like, it could be any day now, really. I've been having contractions and everything."

Summer hasn't been to school for the last two months. I know it stresses her out, and the pursed look she gets whenever I talk about school makes me realise just how much she's holding back. I want to talk to her about it, to ask her what the plan is, but I don't want to push her over the edge. She still has so much to focus on, and it's so easy for school to get lost in the mix on insanity.

"Well, you should just stay here while Jackson and I go to look at that apartment this afternoon. I don't want you giving birth in our potential new house," I snort.

"You really think this one could be it? God, I don't want to even get my hopes up anymore. I'm so sick of being let down."

"I don't know," I answer. "I do like the look of it and the price is right. Which means there's probably something horribly wrong with it. Either way, Jackson and I will check it out. You just focus on you."

"That's all I've been doing for the past eight weeks. Like, I really am just so impatient to meet her. And get everything all sorted. Our house, our future...it really is going to work out. I know it."

"How do you know it?" I ask quietly, finally letting my vulnerability slip through my words. It's been a tumultuous few days, and the stormy uncertainty that has been clouding around me seems to seep through every aspect of my life. "How do you know everything is going to work out? RMIT rejected me, we don't have proper jobs...everything is so uncertain."

"It is," she agrees. "But I don't think you'll be worrying about having a job for much longer."

I raise my eyebrows. "What?"

"I think Jackson should tell you..." she says slowly, pressing her lips together to suppress a smile. "Look, just have faith that everything *will* work out. We'll figure it out."

I want to argue with her, make her tell me whatever secret she's hiding...but my poor best friend is thirty-six weeks pregnant and the last thing she needs is me pestering her.

"I'm glad I got to talk to Kat yesterday," I say, changing the subject. "She has helped so much. After the fight with Amber, I honestly feel like I'm just going to give up on love for good."

Summer grins at me. "Maybe it's right in front of you." She winks, obviously referring to Kat. "But she's right, you know. You do need to give up on the drinking and partying for a while—and I'm not just saying that because I'm jealous, because I'm not! I just want you to find happiness, and that environment isn't healthy. You saw it with Amber—it just causes conflict."

"To be fair, I think the conflict with Amber was inevitable." I sigh. "It was bound to happen. There was so much anger and frustration. I just wish it was different." My voice begins to shake a little bit, and I swallow hard. "I wish we could've been friends."

"There's still a chance," Summer says.

"I don't think so. I think that's it. Even if I wanted to work things out with her, I don't think she'd want anything to do with me. And that's that."

"That's that," Summer echoes. "What about Kat, though?" Her eyebrows are raised expectantly, and she's got a mischievous smile dancing across her full lips.

"What about her?" I ask innocently, but my heart is fluttering. I know exactly what Summer is insinuating, and...I can't really deny it. "No, but really. It is what it is. I don't know what is going to happen with Kat. She's been amazing. She's put up with my craziness. She's incredible."

"Do you like her?"

I hesitate, pressing my lips together as I consider her question. "I don't know. Maybe I do."

"She likes you."

The fire rips across my cheeks, and butterflies dance through my stomach at the thought of that. I know that's what she said a while ago, but a lot has changed since then. I've made a lot of mistakes.

"Maybe."

Summer strokes her stomach as she sits cross-legged on her bed. Every time she touches her stomach, she looks like she has no other cares in the world. I've heard about all the gross stuff, all the painful stuff, that she's had to go through with this pregnancy. I've seen every time she's had to puke into a restaurant bin, every time she's had to stop in the middle of the road screaming at me to find the closest bathroom. But the smile that lights up her features shows me that it's worth every second.

"God, I feel so caught up in the middle," Summer says. "Like, one part of me still feels like I'm seventeen, you know? I feel like I'm just a kid, talking about crushes and school. On the other hand, I'm a mum. Already, I feel like a mum. I am so damn protective of Adeline. If anything were to happen to her..." She chokes up, and I'm surprised at the intensity of the emotion in her voice. It's something I can't possibly comprehend yet. I'm just not at that level. "It's so weird, Ingrid. I feel so alone."

I'm shocked at her confession. This is the first time I've heard about it, and my heart falters. I feel guilty for never asking. I was being selfish; I was only thinking about myself.

"You're not alone," I gasp. "You'll never be alone. You have me and Jackson. We're here for you always."

"I know, I know," Summer says shakily. "I can't explain it. I feel like I'm just being hormonal and crazy. I just feel like my mind is going to explode. There is *so* much going on, so much to think about and...I feel like it's all in my hands. I know it's not. I know you guys are here for me. I just feel crazy."

"Oh, Sum." I sigh, wrapping my arms around her shoulders. "If there is anything I can do to help, if I can make you feel better at all...please let me know."

"Just don't let me do this alone," she whispers, blinking rapidly. For the first time in a long time, I see the fear in her eyes, I see the worries she has to face. "Promise me you'll be here."

"I'll be here forever. I promise."

"LOOK, I REALLY want to let you know what's going on before we go into this apartment," Jackson says, tearing up blades of grass and throwing them to the side. I've seen him fidget when he's nervous before, but as I stare up at the cloudless blue sky, I wonder what on earth he has to be nervous about.

"Why do I feel like this is going to be bad?" I ask, desperately attempting to keep my calm. I don't know why I'm being so pessimistic. I'm just expecting the worst all of the time.

"It's not," Jackson shakes his head. "I'm just...nervous. I don't want to get my hopes up."

"I know the feeling," I mutter, knowing that my hesitation to get my hopes up has nothing to do with what Jackson is worried about.

"I think...I think I may have found us a job," he announces, turning to face me expectantly. "I don't want you to freak out and get excited, but I contacted a publisher of that monthly literary magazine and...he needs artists."

"We're students," I say bluntly, feeling immediately terrified. "He'd want volunteers."

"If we're up to his standards, he's willing to pay us minimum wage. That's better than nothing."

"That's better than I could've even imagined..." I breathe. "Like, really? We could be paid for art?"

Jackson nods enthusiastically. "At this stage, he wants us to send him our portfolios and let him know what we enjoy doing and what we're good at. We've got such distinctly different styles that it could really work to our advantage, Ingrid. I think we could really have a chance here."

"I'm so sick of being let down," I whisper. "I don't want this to fall through. I don't want to miss out, Jacks. This is really amazing. We could get this because of you."

"We could," Jackson says proudly. "So, here's the plan. We're going to go to look at this apartment, love it, put in our application, and get it. Then we're going to work on our portfolios and submit them and start earning money for our art."

"And somewhere in between that, you're going to have a baby."

"And graduate high school," Jackson adds, widening his eyes.

"And figure out what we're doing with our lives." I smirk.

"And find you a wifey."

We are wheezing with laughter. We collapse onto the grass, gripping our stomachs with tears streaming down our faces. The laughter crashes through my body, washing away the anxiety and fears. We've got so much happening, and a lot of it is scary, a lot of it is terrifying, but some of it is amazing.

"Thanks." I grin. "For making me feel better and giving me a little perspective."

Jackson nudges my shoulder, still smiling. "I mean it, though; we are going to find you a wifey. Unless you've already found one?"

I smirk at him, standing up and pulling him up with me. "Maybe I have." I wink. "Come on, let's go and look at this apartment because it really is too good to be true."

It is true, though.

The apartment is amazing. Kind of small, but perfect for the three—soon to be four—of us. Three bedrooms, nice little kitchen. A small balcony. I can already imagine myself sitting out on the balcony in the morning with my coffee and a sketchbook. It's perfect.

"God, not even a weird smell!" Jacksons says as we exit the apartment. "Just watch, we'll have our application rejected immediately."

"It is likely we'll get rejected," I agree, trying to control my hope. "We just have to be patient. We'll apply and see what happens. If we get rejected, we'll keep looking. Simple."

Jackson sighs, running a hand through his messy curls. "I really want it, though. It would be perfect for us. I know Summer would love it too. And Adeline."

"Look, let's just put in our application and see what happens."

"I'm just so hopeful," Jackson whispers.

"Me too."

Chapter Sixteen

I DON'T KNOW why I feel awkward as I grip my glass of wine. Maybe it's because this restaurant is too fancy or because my dress is too tight, but as Kat watches me with an amused smile dancing across her bright red lips, I feel lost for words.

The soft acoustic music lilting through the low-lit restaurant reminds me of Amber, and I shove that thought away angrily. I don't want to think about her. Tonight is about Kat.

"Now *this* is a good way to enjoy alcohol."

"Is that the only reason you chose this restaurant?" I smirk, meeting TJ's eyes across the room. It's strange to see him without his brightly coloured headscarf and dreadlocks. His hair is smoothed tightly behind his neck, and his suit is tight and muted. "Because you knew TJ would be here to sneak us drinks?"

"No." Kat laughs unconvincingly. "Okay, maybe a little. Just a drink—to ease the nerves."

"You're nervous?" I ask quietly.

"A little. Are you?"

"Yeah."

For a moment, we just watch each other. I realise that I've been biting my lip this whole time. I take a deep breath, trying to regain my confidence. This is a date. There's no denying it. The truth is, it's exactly what I wanted. This is what I want.

Boldly, I reach across the table and stroke my fingers along her bare arm. She looks incredible in her flowing navy dress. Her hair is tied up in a loose bun on the top of her head.

A soft chuckle escapes her lips, and she visibly relaxes. I fall into this rare moment of blissful happiness. There are so many things to look forward to right now. I have so much to be thankful for. Right now, sitting opposite Kat is all I could ever ask for. This is perfect.

Throughout dinner, I tell her about the apartment, the possible job...everything. I just keep talking. I'm pretty sure Kat doesn't even get a word in. The smile that beams from her face tells me that she doesn't mind it at all.

TJ grins at us from across the restaurant, giving us the thumbs-up every now and then. The night is perfect. We laugh and talk, and suddenly, there is no pressure. I'm not scared anymore. I'm not worried. I'm just enjoying this moment in all of its simplicity.

After the restaurant, we walk down the street holding hands. I don't know who reaches out first, but we entwine our fingers and Kat's thumb smoothly brushes across the back of my hand. I'm avidly listening as she tells me stories from her wild days—which weren't that long ago.

"You don't really have any crazy stories, do you?"

"The only wild days I've had are since you came into my life. Not that I'm complaining."

"It's so funny that since meeting you, I've become less wild and you've become more wild." She chuckles. "It's like we're kind of meeting in the middle."

"I like that." I sigh, stopping to lean against one of the trees that line this little street. There are fairy lights twinkling, and I am feeling lost in the perfectness of our little moment. "I like you..."

Kat's smile shines through the darkness.

I reach out, wrap my arms around her waist, and slip my fingers along the flowing fabric of her dress. I pull her body closer to mine, and our foreheads fall against each other. She brushes her fingers along my cheek before reaching behind my neck and pulling my face forward.

Before I know it, our lips barely touch. Then they brush against each other ever so slightly, and I fall head first into this moment. I kiss her softly as the intensity smoulders within me.

She curls her fingers into my hair, stroking the back of my neck.

As we stand in the dark street under the twinkling lights, falling into our quiet little kiss, I capture this moment in my memory, making sure to remind myself of every breath that escapes Kat's lips, of every breeze that tickles against my bare arms, of every curve on Kat's body.

This is happiness.

JACKSON IS STILL waiting up when I get home. He smiles from ear to ear as I tell him in hushed whispers about my date with Kat, desperately trying not to wake my parents.

"Why did you wait up?" I ask him after I've exhausted all possible talk of my date. There's only so many times I can talk about the "spark" before Jackson melts into the ground with boredom.

"I feel like something's gonna happen tonight," he says with wide eyes. "I feel like tonight's the night."

"What do you mean?"

"With Addie. I feel like she's going to come tonight. Dad's instinct."

I snort into my hands, trying not to offend Jackson. "I feel like Summer is the only one that gets to play that card." I chuckle. "And technically, it's already tomorrow. So we'll see."

"Should we place a bet?" Jackson asks eagerly.

"You want to place a bet on the birth of your daughter? Oh, Jacks, your age is really showing now."

"I'm excited!" he argues. "This is the start of my life."

"You're not scared?"

"Of course I am," he answers without hesitation. "Absolutely terrified. That doesn't mean I can't be excited, though. And I'm telling you, it's gonna happen. Tonight, today, *soon*."

"One hundred dollars." I smirk. "That'll be enough for me to get some nice new bed sheets for our new apartment."

My comment makes Jackson smile even more—it shows that I'm hopeful about this apartment too. All I want is for our application to be accepted and everything to fall into place. We've worked so hard to get to this point.

"Deal." He reaches out and shakes my hand. "She's coming, Ingrid. I can feel it."

"Well, if that is the case, I'm going to have to go to bed and emotionally prepare myself for what is probably going to be the most terrifying experience of my life," I say. "And maybe dissect every single moment of that date."

SUMMER SPENDS THE day at my house with Jackson and me, looking through pictures of what could be our future apartment, talking about the plans that Jackson and I have for our portfolio.

All day, Summer is uncomfortable. She grips her stomach and pants through contractions as I stand by awkwardly, feeling helpless. Jackson rubs her backs, shooting me hopeful looks. It's starting to look like his crazy "Dad instinct" might actually be right.

We decide to have Summer stay over for the night, since we're hoping to hear about the apartment tomorrow. My mum constantly asks Summer questions, trying to determine if she should stay home tonight—she and Dad were planning on taking the weekend to go out of town, and naturally, she is concerned that we have no idea what we're doing when it comes to Summer giving birth.

Summer refuses to let my mum stay—insisting that she enjoys her weekend away and Summer is in good hands. At the end of the day, I don't want my parents missing out on a weekend away just because of the small chance that Summer could be giving birth.

So, we say goodbye to my parents and drag all of the mattresses into the lounge room to watch bad reality television shows. Jackson shovels chips into his mouth and talks about his latest comic book idea—an invisible superhero who befriends lonely kids, which isn't actually as creepy as it sounds—when Summer starts moaning again.

"It's worse this time." She gasps through the contractions. "I feel like they're getting worse."

My heart is in my throat because my instincts were telling me to convince my parents to stay, but I ignored them. This could actually be happening, and I have no idea what to do. I realise that maybe it would've been better for me to go to those birthing classes because I know that Jackson wasn't listening to a word they were telling him.

"We should start timing them," I insist, trying to remember everything I've ever seen or read about giving birth. "I don't know… How fast are they meant to come?"

Summer's response is a guttural moan as she grips her stomach, staring down and squeezing her eyes shut.

"I'm going to call the hospital." Jackson's voice is breathy, and his eyes are as wide as saucers as he searches for his phone.

"No," Summer moans. "There's no time. We have to go."

My heart is pounding as my mind spins into overdrive. How is this happening so fast? How did this all fall apart so quickly? One minute, we were eating chips and complaining about how unrealistic reality television is, and the next, Adeline is on her way. What do I do?

"Okay," I say, quickly jumping to my feet. "I'm going to get the keys. Do you have your bags?"

"Yes, at the door," Jackson gasps, helping Summer to her feet. She is almost doubled over, gripping her massive stomach and moaning loudly. "Come on, we have to go."

"Get me to the hospital!" Summer yells, her voice cracking with the pain.

I rip my handbag open, upturning the contents of it onto the lounge room floor. There is lipstick, empty chip wrappers, water bottles flying everywhere. I throw the contents away, finally finding my car keys.

"Let's go, let's go!" I shout. I run out to the front door and open all of my car doors as quickly as possible. Jackson half drags Summer out the front door as she moans through the contractions. He lowers her into the back seat and slams the door shut. His eyes are wild, and his hands fly everywhere as he tries to keep up with the situation.

Before I know it, we are on the road. I drive as fast as is safe and desperately try to remember everything I ever knew about what to do when someone is in labour. "Has her water broken?" I shout into the back seat, tapping my hand impatiently against the steering wheel. My only goal is to get Summer to the hospital as quickly as possible.

"It's kind of like she wet her pants," Jackson says breathlessly. "So I think that's a yes."

I don't even care about my car seats or the potential fact that Summer may have actually wet her pants. I just press my foot down a little harder on the accelerator. I need to get my best friend to safety. I can't let her give birth on the back seat of my car. This isn't how it's meant to be.

Suddenly, my phone rings and Summer screams loudly.

"Go faster, Ingrid!" Jackson bellows. His voice explodes in my ear, and I push my beat-up Nissan to its limits, driving faster than I thought it was possible in this piece of junk.

The streets are deserted, and my low-beam headlights aren't giving me enough vision for the speeds that I'm driving. Summer's screams become more intense, and I flick on my high-beams. I need to get to the hospital. I can't let her down. I promised I'd be there for her.

My tires screech as I round the corners. We're on the home stretch now—less than ten minutes away from the hospital.

"Ingrid, please," Summer gasps from the back seat in between her guttural moans. "Hurry up."

I rev my car into top gear, pushing it to the limits. My eyes flicker to my speedometer as it creeps up past the legal limit. The temperature gauge is hitting high levels too. Surely if the police pull me over, I have a valid reason? Summer could be giving birth any minute, and it's past midnight, so there is no one else on the roads.

Oh, it's past midnight. I guess Jackson didn't win the bet after all—I make a mental note to laugh at him as soon as we get to the hospital safely.

That is the last coherent thought I have before everything comes to a screaming halt. It's a squeal of tires, a blowing horn, and a deafening crash that stops everything.

Someone once told me that when you panic, everything goes into hyper speed. I can't remember who said it—probably my mother—but they couldn't be more wrong.

Everything moves at a quarter of an inch per second. I see everything so clearly. I don't know if it's the blinding high-beam lights reflecting from the silver car that cuts the corner onto the road in front of us or the fact that everything has snapped into focus, but suddenly, everything is startlingly, terrifyingly clear.

Jackson's frantic yell is drowned out by Summer's continuous moaning. I slam on the brakes, but my foot moves too slowly. I can't catch up. The moment barrels towards me and I'm screaming and bracing myself, but I'm not fast enough.

I'll never be fast enough.

My tires squeal and swerve from side to side, and I spin the wheel, desperately trying to keep up. I can't keep up.

I scrunch my eyes shut, willing for a pause. Praying for the moment to stop, for everything to stop. It won't stop, though. Nothing can stop.

The sickening sound of metal on metal meets me before the pain does. One hot flash, one strangled scream, and everything is black.

Chapter Seventeen

"INGRID SUSTAINED THE worst of the injuries."

The words scream into my aching skull, halting every hope I have of falling into blissful unawareness. It penetrates me, stabbing me with hot, fiery pokers. I can't feel anything but this sharp pain in my head. I can't think of anything but—

"Summer!" The strangled voice that breaks through the wave of screaming words has to be mine, but it doesn't sound like mine. I want to scream; I want to sob. I want to find my best friend.

I can't see anything. The world is a mess of blurred, muted colours, and I can't comprehend my existence aside from the dead cold fear that washes over me as the thought of Summer flashes through my mind.

"Summer is okay. So are Adeline and Jackson."

I don't know who's speaking, and I can't quite comprehend the enormity of what they are saying because the stabbing pain moves from my head to the rest of my body. My entire body is on fire, and I want nothing more than to escape into the darkness. I can't shut it out. An incessant beeping drills into my skull, and there is a harsh buzz in front of my eyes. With every ounce of strength remaining in my exhausted body, I wrench them open.

"Ingrid, honey, you need to relax." It's a calm voice beside me that speaks. Soft like silk. If I could wrap myself up in that voice and fall asleep in it, I would be the happiest girl in the world.

"You've been out for hours," a harsher voice tells me. "If you can open your eyes, I can begin the examination."

The harsh buzz in front of my eyes appears to be the fluorescent lights that fill this white room. I can't move. I can hardly breathe. Everything is too much. The lights, the voices, the machine noises. I can't focus on the bodies that fill this room. I can't focus on anything but the bright white ceiling.

"You've received severe head trauma in your car crash, Ingrid," the harsh voice tells me. "I'm here with your friend Kat, and your parents are on their way. I have Doctor Abraham with me to assist me with the post-surgery examination."

Questions pound through me, and I realise that the silk voice must have been Kat's. I wish I could see her; I wish I could meet her eyes. I can't see anyone.

"When we arrived at the scene, your friend Summer was giving birth and her partner, Jackson, was assisting at the scene. He had also pulled you out of the car and to safety, adding to trauma in your spine and nerves near your brain. We had to undertake emergency surgery to protect the exposed nerves and clear out bone fragments in your wrist and forearm. You will be in an extended cast for at least a month."

I gasp for air, flickering my eyes, trying to gain control of my uncooperative body. I want to speak; I want to see what's going on. I want to breathe.

"Maybe you can tell her this later?" It's Kat who speaks now, and I want to fall into her and let her beautiful voice swirl around me. I want to fall into her comfort.

"I'll just do this examination, and we'll leave you with her." A new voice speaks—a man with a low, guttural tone that seems to get straight to the point.

The room seems to spin, and I feel disjointed as cold hands prod my skin and sharp needles sting my arms. I breathe slowly, waiting for everything to snap into focus as the bodies lean over me, reminding me that I have no control over anything right now.

Gradually, the faces become clearer. A chubby man stands over me, shining a light into my eyes, and a skinny woman with an angular nose presses her hands on my chest. I flicker my gaze to the person next to me, just out of my line of vision. It's Kat. She slides her chair forward, resting her hands on my free arm. Her eyes are wide with dark bags almost down to her cheeks. I try to speak, but my mouth is so dry.

"It looks like she's doing well after the surgery," the chubby doctor says. "We'll just take some blood and be back in four hours."

A final prick in my aching arm and a shuffle of feet and I am alone in the room with Kat's soft breathing beside me.

"Ingrid..." Her voice shakes, and I want to wrap my arms around her. I want to kiss her and tell her that I'm okay, but I'm still frozen, trapped on this uncomfortable bed with my dry lips and aching head. "It's okay. Everyone is okay. Jackson called me as soon as he was cleared. He doesn't even have a scratch on him, the bastard."

"Summer..." My voice is clearer now. It's hoarse and dry, but I am finally in control of the words. Her name is all I can manage, though.

"Summer and Adeline are doing great," Kat says, and although her face blurs in and out of focus, I can hear the smile in her voice. "The other driver is also okay."

"Surgery," I gasp, wheezing out the word as I desperately try to keep up with the stream of information.

"You're okay, Ingrid," Kat reassures me. "Just focus on that. Now, be quiet and let me hold your hand. Go back to sleep. I'll be here. I'll always be here."

OUR HORRIFYING NIGHT looks even scarier in the stark light of day. My whole body aches, and as I sleepily examine the cast on my right arm, Kat stirs in the seat beside me. My attention turns to her, and as I watch her, the pain in my body seems to subside just a little.

The memories of last night come back in horrific flashes. It feels like a hangover but one million times worse. I cringe away as I recall the moment my car collided with the oncoming car. The sickening screech of brakes, the squeal of metal on metal... I shudder and thrust the memories away.

With my nonplastered hand, I reach out and wrap my fingers around Kat's. I don't know how I would've made it through the night without her—even between the nurses coming in every four hours, she refused to leave.

She stretches out and a soft sigh escapes her lips. Her eyes flutter open and she smiles at me.

"Good morning," she says sleepily.

"Hi," I breathe.

"How are you feeling?"

"I'm fine." The words come easier this morning. My voice is still hoarse and my mouth is still desperately dry, but I can finally speak full sentences. "What about Summer and Jackson? Adeline?"

"They're doing great," Kat says. "Jackson will probably be in later if he can tear himself away from Summer. She's just got to have some extra rest since it was kind of a traumatic delivery, but it sounds like Jackson did an amazing job."

"And I was just a mess." I sigh. "I fucked up."

"No you didn't," Kat reassures me, squeezing my hand. "Ingrid, it could've happened to anyone. You did everything you could and you were under a lot of pressure."

"Mum's gonna kill me," I say, my voice wavering. "God, I'm a bad friend."

"Ingrid, shut up. You're incredible," Kat tells me. "Everyone is okay...well, except you, I guess. And your car."

I roll my eyes. "That's the last of my worries. I don't care if I'm not okay—I deserve it."

Boldly, Kat reaches out and presses her lips softly against mine. She tangles her hand through my hair and strokes her fingers along my cheek. I smile against her lips. I'm now certain that this eases the pain in my wrecked body.

"Well, it looks like your lips still work, even if your arm is fucked."

I try to laugh, but my body aches and it stays stuck in my chest. "How am I going to draw?" I ask croakily. "My portfolio..."

"Ingrid, please stop worrying," Kat pleads. "It's killing me to see you in pain. I want to make everything better for you. I want to help."

"You are helping."

"Tell me what I can do to help you," she continues. "I just want make you feel better."

"I think I've got an idea..."

"What is it?" Kat asks hopefully.

"You could start by kissing me again..."

MY MUM IS almost inconsolable. But as I explain to her everything I can remember, the beginning touches of pride shine across her face. She understands that it was a freak situation. She's not angry. She's glad that we are all okay. That's all that matters.

She asks me about Kat—who has finally gone home to shower after spending all night with me—and her smile is genuine when I finally tell her that I think I'm falling for her. I can't imagine ever keeping anything like this from her.

Jackson interrupts our conversation, and the first thing I note is that Kat was absolutely right—he doesn't have a scratch on him. The second thing I note is the huge out-of-place smile on his lips.

Mum leaves us alone, mentioning something about finding me "proper food," even though I haven't been cleared to eat yet.

"You look extra chirpy for someone who was in a car crash last night," I say through my dry lips.

"I'm a dad. I'm the happiest man alive." Jackson smiles, rubbing my shoulder. "But that's not just why I'm smiling."

"Why are you smiling then?"

"We got the apartment." He beams. "We got it."

I want to let out a squeal, jump with joy, and high-five him all at once. I want to celebrate. But my broken body remains still on this firm hospital bed, and the only thing I can do to show Jackson my enthusiasm is let out a happy squeak and a beaming smile.

"I can't believe it."

"You still want to live with us, right? Because we're going to have a squishy, black-haired, squawking baby with us now."

I beam at him. "Of course I do! I want to meet her."

"She's got to stay with the doctors for a little while longer, just for observation. Don't worry. You'll be seeing a lot of her very soon. She had a pretty traumatic welcome to the world."

"She did," I agree.

"Summer did amazing," he says in awe. "I can't believe how strong she is."

"How is she doing?"

"She's all right...considering. It's not just the car crash that she has to recover from, but the birth as well. I think it's safe to say that you are both going to be out of action for the move."

"I'm sure we've got a few people who can help us out. Did you know that Kat was here all night with me?"

"I do because I called her," Jackson reminds me.

"Oh yeah." I remember, shaking my head at my poor memory. I guess a car crash can have that effect. "Thank you."

Jackson shrugs. "Summer had me. You needed your person."

"I guess she is my person," I agree.

"And she loves you."

I laugh, embarrassed. Jackson still smiles knowingly at me when the doctors walk in. I'm getting used to the interruptions now. Being poked and pricked and prodded, having my temperature, blood pressure, and incision wounds checked. It's no wonder I can't think straight. I'm exhausted.

"We have the police outside," the doctor says. "They just want to ask you a few questions and let you know what's going on, Ingrid. Do you feel up for a conversation?"

I nod, swallowing my fear.

Jackson follows the doctors out of the room, shooting me one last reassuring look before he is replaced by two police officers with pursed lips.

"Hello, Ingrid," the older woman says, folding her arms across her chest. "How are you feeling?"

"I'm okay," I answer croakily. "How can I help you?"

"We just wanted to let you know about what's going to happen after last night's collision," the officer says. "Thankfully, no one was seriously injured, and Miss Stevens and her daughter are doing well too. We wanted to talk to you about the possibility of pressing charges against the driver of the Honda sedan."

"What? They want to press charges?"

My heart is thundering. I hadn't considered this possibility, but I know that it's something that I deserve.

"No, Ingrid," the officer says. "You have the right to press charges against him. He did have alcohol in his blood—although he was just under the legal limit. This is an option for you and something you should consider carefully."

"No way. It was a freak accident. Everyone is safe, and most importantly, Summer and Adeline are okay. I know that I was driving fast. I was panicking and needed to get her to the hospital."

The police officer nods once. "We understand. We just had to let you know of the possible outcomes of this situation. We'll leave you to think about it, and you are more than welcome to contact us if you have any questions."

"Thank you," I say.

The police officers leave me alone in the small hospital room, and my mind is reeling. I don't care about pressing charges or the outcomes of this car crash. I'm just glad that everyone is okay. All I can think about is getting out of this hospital room and returning to my normal life.

I chuckle to myself when I realise that I don't know what normal is anymore.

Chapter Eighteen

"IF THERE WAS anyone who could find a way to get out of the heavy lifting, it'd be you." Leon grins, flopping down on the grass beside me. "If you get to lie out here and get a tan, then I'm gonna lie with you."

"You're black. You don't need a tan." I snort. "But I'm more than happy to have the company."

"How long do you have to wear that number for?" he asks, nodding to the vivid pink cast that encases my right arm from my wrist to my upper arm.

"Who knows?" I ask. "I feel like every time I go back to a doctor, they tell me there's something else wrong with me. I've decided to stop caring. That car crash really messed me up."

"You may be physically messed up, but you seem happier. Which is kind of weird."

"I was never normal. But I guess you're right. I can deal with being physically messed up if it means my mind is clear. The whole moving-out thing has helped a little too."

"And Kat."

"Yes, and Kat."

Leon nudges me. "Well, if you could've figured that out about three months ago, that would've saved you a whole lotta heartbreak. But hey, just ignore me."

"Oh well. That's life."

"I guess it is…"

I pick at my pink cast as Jackson and my dad drag boxes into our little apartment. It's that time of day when the sun seems infinite in its blaze. It bores down on us, highlighting the buzz of productivity that happens between the large moving van parked on the street and our little front door.

With some help from Jackson, I managed to pull together some of my better sketches and my RMIT portrait draft to submit to the publisher.

I felt completely inadequate when I saw my portfolio compared to the crazy comic that Jackson had produced. I turn to Leon, suddenly realising that he had never gotten to see the comic.

"You know Jackson made a comic based on you?" I ask, smiling.

"Bullshit," Leon scoffs.

"Seriously," I answer. "At first, we talked about a black superhero, and then we talked about Jackson's unique comic ideas, and it just kind of happened... You know how you have this way of just understanding people? Well, Jackson came up with a little boy superhero who could read minds. He ends up having to go on a mission to save his classmates from an evil bus driver. You definitely need to see it."

Leon laughs so hard tears glint in his eyes, and I don't know whether it's from humour or happiness or both. "That's amazing," he says. "Is it any good?"

"It's amazing," I gush. "Seriously, comparing what I do to what he can do makes me feel like shit. I feel so inadequate next to him."

It's easy to tell Leon how I feel. I've been through so much with him already, and he seems to just...get people, which is kind of where Jackson's comic came from.

"Oh, Ingrid, cut the crap." Leon rolls his eyes. "You don't need to make everything about you. Both you and Jackson are great artists, but you're completely different. You make beautiful, pretty things that forty-year-old women want to hang on their walls. Jackson wants to connect with vulnerable children. They're two completely different things. You can't compare it."

"I guess you're right." I sigh.

"You do need to stop doing that," Leon chastises me. "You compare yourself to everyone. Amber, Kat, Summer, Jackson. Just stop. You are you. Just be the most authentic version of yourself that you can be, and you can succeed at anything."

I taste Leon's words on my tongue as I consider them. All I ever wanted was to be authentic. I just wanted to be my true self. In searching for her, I lost myself. Leon's right. I was just comparing myself to what I thought I should be. I got so lost in my ways that I couldn't see who she was.

"Have I ever told you that I love you?" I ask genuinely. "Seriously, I have no idea what I'd do without you, Leon."

"Ingrid Harper, you are a hot mess, and I wouldn't have it any other way."

I AM CURLED up on the couch with Kat while Summer and Jackson fuss over Adeline when it happens.

Kat stops twirling her fingers through my hair, and Jackson whips his head up. My stomach drops, and immediately, I manoeuvre my body so I can grab my phone with my working arm. The *ding* of an email seems to have silenced the whole room. Even Adeline stops whining and makes quiet little baby noises.

"Is it him?" Summer asks. Her voice has snapped out of its high-pitched baby voice and is suddenly flat and serious.

It feels like our future is riding on this email. Logically, I know that if things don't work out, then we'll figure something else out. I've already been taking on shifts at the local library just to make sure we're covered for this move, but it's not enough. This could be the opportunity that changes everything.

"It's him," I gasp, unlocking my phone with shaking fingers. The breath has escaped my chest, and my thundering heart can't seem to keep up with the burst of adrenaline that pounds through my body. "The publisher."

"Oh god, don't tell me," Jackson moans, clenching his fists and closing his eyes.

Summer pulls Adeline onto her chest, burying her head in her chest as if her two-month-old daughter will protect her from the answers that this email holds.

"I can't look," I breathe.

"Oh for fuck's sake." Kat sighs, snatching my phone from me. "You're all acting like babies. Even Addie is embarrassed for you."

"Language!" Jackson chides, seemingly forgetting about the heaviness of this moment.

"Hi, Ingrid and Jackson. Thank you for your portfolio submissions," Kat reads out loud. Our attention snaps to her, and we wait for her next sentence with bated breath. "Jackson, I really enjoyed your unique comic idea and I am looking forward to seeing what you come up with next. Ingrid, you show promise with your sketches and I applaud your ability to provide your portfolio, given the circumstances..." Kat pauses, glancing up at me. Our gazes meet, and immediately, I know what the next sentences say. My heart thunders, and I grip Kat's leg tightly. "It's my pleasure to offer you both entry-level positions at *The Grasshopper*. Please call me later and we will discuss contract details."

"Oh my god," I squeal, falling back as Kat throws my phone to the side and jumps on top of me.

She leans over and attacks me with kisses all over my face. "Oh, I'm just so proud of you," she says, mimicking Summer's baby voice. "You did it!"

"*We* did it." I smile over at Jackson who is hugging Summer and Adeline. There are tears trickling down her rosy cheeks.

"Damn pregnancy hormones," she mutters, kissing Adeline's forehead. "Oh, guys, I'm so happy. Now I just need to get a job."

"You'll get there. I think you've kind of got your hands full at the minute."

"I suppose I do..." Summer says airily, nuzzling her head into his neck. "And I've got my end-of-year coursework to catch up on."

"Exactly," Kat says from beside me. "Speaking of which...Ingrid, did you want to show me that book of yours?"

I raise my eyebrows at her expectantly. "Sure..." I say, then take her hand and follow her into my new bedroom. Jackson snorts as we leave the room.

"So, I have a book to show you...?" I giggle, clicking the door shut behind me. Kat chuckles, entwining her fingers through mine.

"Oh, it's a pretty interesting book..." she purrs, then presses her lips against my neck.

She leans her body against mine and kisses me slowly. Every move is deliberate and teasing as she kisses me. I wrap my arms around her neck, manoeuvring my cast over her shoulder, and she grips my waist and curls her fingers under the waistband of my jeans, then flicks her tongue across my lips, sealing the kiss.

"Only you could make a cast looks sexy," she murmurs against my lips, accentuating every word with a light kiss.

"Only you could find a cast sexy." I laugh, deepening the kiss.

With great restraint, she pulls away. She grabs my good hand and leads me to the bed, a flirty smile dancing across her lips.

We fall back onto the bed, giggling as our limbs curl around each other. She kisses me hard, letting out little gasps as her tongue encircles mine and her hands roam my body. Cast or no cast, there is nowhere I would rather be.

I'M FROZEN ON my stool.

My mind spins as the lyrics surround me. All I can do is study the pink cast on my arm, pick at a stray thread, and chew my lips. The beautiful melody is enthralling. The softly strewn rhythm dances through the air, capturing the attention of every person in this crowded bar.

The drunken men and older women ignore the tears splattering down my cheeks. Amber sings softly, gripping the microphone stand as she caresses the words that escape from her talented lips. She slowly builds up to the crescendo. Her words grow stronger as she reaches the climax. Her eyes flutter shut as she draws out every lyric, her tone falling deeper and deeper.

I cry in earnest now, trying not to draw attention to myself as I hold the tissue to my nose. Amber hasn't seen me—or if she has, she pretended not to—and that's exactly how I wanted it. Around me, there are mutters of praise. I want to tell them to shut up and listen to her voice because Amber Freeman has a voice that can stop the world.

She sings for every word that wasn't said, sings for every person that was ever silenced. She sings for the scared little girls and lonely little boys. As Amber sings, everything snaps into focus. The crowd becomes vibrant in their responses. Women sway along with her voice. Men close their eyes as they listen, falling into every lilted tone and cascading lyric. People record her, mouths open in awe as they turn to raise their eyebrows at their friends, impressed.

Her talent is undeniable as the climax of the song comes crashing down and her voice trickles through the wave of emotions without falter. I wipe my tears away as her voice heals me, just the way it heals everyone. I'm not the only one crying anymore. She has a special way of throwing us into the moment—*her* moment—and letting the tension, pain and frustration of life fall away.

As she sings, I let go of every hurtful argument, of every murmur of disappointment that crashed between us. I always knew that Amber Freeman was something special. There was something so undeniably curious about her. She has a way of clumsily crashing through the world, whilst also managing to sing with such grace and delicacy. I always knew that I wanted to be her friend.

Amber is *so* important. It may have been Kat who helped me come to terms with my sexuality, and in the end, I was the only person who could work through my own identity, but...Amber is something different. She always was.

I never wanted things to turn sour with Amber like they did, and even looking back on what happened between us, I can't quite pinpoint where it all fell apart. Maybe Amber did things wrong, but so did I. We are flawed people, and I don't know how to fix that.

Her voice connects my thoughts to my feelings, and I realise that it doesn't matter anymore. It doesn't matter because I am human and so is Amber. We are just broken humans who are looking to find our way in the world.

Aren't we all just broken?

Amber finishes her set to thundering applause. She beams as she stares out into the crowd, thanking them with a shy voice. As soon as she finishes singing, it's like she transforms into a different person—a little self-conscious, a little shy, but more than aware of her ability to capture the attention of a crowded room with just her voice.

Without thinking, I am on my feet, screaming and shouting my applause. My voice is strangled, and I know that my mascara is leaking onto my cheeks. The people around me probably think that I am crazy, but I don't care. I won't hide my appreciation.

I won't hide anymore.

Amber's gaze flickers over to me and widens for just a second, shocked. My smile widens, and I start laughing as I clap for her. Her shoulders slump and the smile breaks across her lips. After thanking the crowd one last time, she walks off the stage, head ducked in appreciation.

I awkwardly make my way through the crowd, trying to avoid whacking people with my giant cast. Amber meets me halfway, still smiling.

"Nice cast." She smirks as a way of greeting. "You're the last person I expected to see here—and that's not because it's a bowls club at four in the afternoon."

I laugh loudly, opening my arms to embrace her. "I promise I won't hit you with it. This cast is a bit of a weapon, you know."

She hugs me tightly, giggling into my shoulder. "I'm glad you came, Ingrid," she breathes. She pulls away, her smiling expression transforming into curiosity. "Uh...why *did* you come?"

"Because Jackson caught me watching your videos again," I answer honestly. "And I'm sick of not talking to you. Shit happened between us, but I want to forget it. You're crazy and talented and interesting, and that happens to be exactly the kind of people I like to have in my life."

Amber grins at me. "Is that a compliment?"

"It's whatever you want it to be."

"Does Kat know you're here?"

"Of course, she does," I tell her. "She would've come along, but she said that power ballads aren't her thing."

"Who doesn't love a power ballad?" Amber laughs.

"I'm working on it, okay?" I roll my eyes. "So, can we just put this past year of bullshit aside and finally be friends? I'm sick of not being able to just turn up at your house and make fun of all the ridiculous stuffed animals on your bed. Not that I've ever done that, but just so you know, I plan to."

"Friends it is," Amber agrees.

The crowd is boisterous around us, empowered by Amber's singing and the cheap alcohol at the bar. We find a pair of stools near the back of the room, and suddenly, I'm telling Amber about everything that I couldn't tell her when we weren't talking.

As we talk, I realise why people fall apart. Sure, we're all broken, but we don't have to be alone. We thrive on the company of people who are just as broken as we are. *That's* why I was always so fascinated by Amber. The thing that ultimately tore us apart is the thing that will keep us together. It is the thing that brings *everyone* together—Summer, Jackson, Leon, Kat, Amber. We are all together.

We are all broken.

About the Author

Gemma is a young Australian author, working as a legal transcriber from home. She loves reading contemporary YA fiction and runs a writing Instagram, where she shares excerpts of her current projects.

Email: gemmgilmore@gmail.com

Twitter: @gemmgilmore

Website: www.instagram.com/writergemm

Also Available from NineStar Press

Connect with NineStar Press

www.ninestarpress.com

www.facebook.com/ninestarpress

www.facebook.com/groups/NineStarNiche

www.twitter.com/ninestarpress

www.tumblr.com/blog/ninestarpress